FEED THEM THEIR OWN

DUSTIN MILLER

Copyright © 2019 Dustin Miller
All rights reserved
First Edition

PAGE PUBLISHING, INC.
Conneaut Lake, PA

First originally published by Page Publishing 2019

ISBN 978-1-64628-709-3 (pbk)
ISBN 978-1-64628-710-9 (digital)

Printed in the United States of America

The Hospital

"Are you going to the hospital today?" were the first words out of my mouth.

I was on the phone with my older sister, Claire. Our uncle, Avery, had been in intensive care after having a severe stroke only a few days before.

"I can't make it this time, Steve. I'm pulling a double. One of the employees came down with something pretty serious I heard, and I'm behind on my rent," she replied.

Claire worked as a waitress, full-time, at a mom-and-pop Mexican food restaurant. Not exactly what she had intended for her life, but she seemed to be content—and I never brought the topic up for discussion.

Knowing that there were no other relatives or close friends in town, I became anxious, realizing that I would be the only one able to make it down there.

"I'm sorry, little bro, but you're going to have to go it alone on this one."

"All right, well, I guess I'll give you a call in the morning to let you know what the latest news is," I said, and we gave our last goodbyes.

"Sounds good, I'll talk to you then. Love ya."

Unenthused, I murmured, "Yeah, love you too, bye," and then tossed the phone to my side after hanging up.

I reluctantly got out of bed and went out into the living room of the one-bedroom apartment I had just moved into a month before. Tiny little cramped place, still crowded with unpacked boxes and all my belongings. But the rent was low, and my neighbors were pleasant enough. I figured that once I had gotten everything unpacked and set up, it would feel more like home—I just wasn't used to the place yet.

Entering the small room, I glanced over at my television but walked past it, knowing that if I had turned it on, it would only prolong the process of getting ready to leave. With the hospital being located in the next town over, the drive usually took about two hours, depending on whether or not you were going to exceed the speed limit of fifty miles per hour, which I usually did.

We had had our fair share of bad experiences with hospitals in the past, my sister and me. Our mother had passed away two years before of cancer. We had practically lived at the damn place—staying overnight, watching over her helplessly and not knowing what might lay ahead, which had gone on for quite a while.

After her passing, I moved in with a couple of friends of mine while still being in a deep depression and not believing that this could ever happen. But I always knew in the back of my mind that one day I would inevitably lose her.

Once I had gotten a stable job, working a forklift in a warehouse, and was able to save up some money, I moved to the other side of town, hoping to escape my own reality; I didn't want to look back, but the whole situation seemed to be repeating itself already—only this time on a smaller scale.

I pulled into the parking lot of the hospital, and the first thing I noticed was the amount of parking spaces available. I had been here several times before, and parking was always an issue, but today was different. I just figured it was a dead time for visitations—no big deal, just seemed strange for this time of day.

I found a parking spot near the front entrance, pulled into it quickly, and parked my truck. As I walked through the entrance doors of the building, that horrible smell came over me. Everyone I had ever talked to about hospitals always mentioned that smell. Sterilization, medical supplies, and even the aroma from the awful cafeteria food seemed to have found its way into the air. It was the morbid contrast between order and death, and it always made me feel a bit uneasy.

There weren't many people roaming the first floor of the hospital, only a handful of nurses, staff, and one janitor minding his own business as he was mopping the floors.

Already feeling uncomfortable, I took a deep breath and quickly made my way toward the elevator, which was located about twenty feet ahead of me. I arrived in front of the two large metal-plated doors and pressed the button to go up. A bell rang, and the doors slid open in front of me. I entered the small, brightly lit space and continued by moving upward to the fourth floor. The bell sounded once more, and the doors opened again. Immediately I could see doctors and nurses moving frantically about, looking over charts, going about their business, seeming to put everything else on hold, focusing on what was most important.

Walking past the other patients' rooms was always one of the hardest parts of coming here. Seeing helpless patients with tubes going into their bodies, family members' looking over their loved ones, not knowing what was going to happen next, and I would always think to myself, *What happened to them? How serious is it? Would this be their last day on earth?* And I would find myself being overtaken by sadness and anxiety. I didn't even know these people, but every family on that floor could relate with one another.

I entered my uncle's room slowly and approached his bedside. "Avery, Uncle Avery, are you awake?" I said to him as he lay nonresponsive in his bed.

The room was stuffy and felt thick with overwhelming heat. I could see the beads of sweat moving slowly down his face. I called a nurse into the room, and a familiar face responded, Brenda. She had been watching over my uncle since he had arrived at the intensive care. A very kind and patient woman who seemed to never let anything bring her down. She left no time available during the day for pessimism to manifest because she knew it only took one small instance of doubt to destroy someone's positive outlook. Any time I visited the hospital, I wondered how anyone could want to become a nurse with all the grief and death that came along with the occupation, but as I thought about it that evening, Brenda began to explain something to me which seemed to solidify her optimistic outlook on the medical field—at least in my eyes.

"You know, usually the family or close friends of the patients ask me how I can do the things I do throughout my long shifts without collapsing or getting overwhelmed and walking out. Every nurse or even doctor I know almost always gets asked that same question or something in that vein, but you haven't said one thing the entire time since you've been coming here," Brenda said, looking at me with a cutesy smirk as she playfully gave me a hard time.

"Well, it's not like I'm not curious. I just figured you get asked those types of questions all the time, it would be like asking a German how they feel about Hitler and the Holocaust," I said and continued. "I guess for me it's a sanitation issue. I don't do well with bodily fluids."

"Ha, ha, ha. Yeah, I figured. Obviously, you've never had kids," said Brenda.

I glanced down at the light reflecting off the tiled floor and shook my head from left to right in embarrassment. To me, it didn't help matters that I looked so young for my age. I was twenty-nine, but appearance-wise, I looked more like I was nineteen. Some said that was a good thing, but I disagreed, feeling as though I was never taken seriously because I was thought of as immature.

Brenda continued to lightly giggle and said, "I have three, and, yes, at first it can be deterring having to clean up bodily fluids from any person, including your own child, but by baby number two, you become desensitized, and those things become second nature. You realize, or at least I did, that caring for a baby becomes a passion but also a full-time job. Baby number one is pretty much played out in a hazy fog. Hardly any sleep and you have no time to stop."

I sat and listened intently.

"The most important thing to do in this field is to sincerely care for the patients and of course keep them alive, monitor them constantly. I can honestly say that I love my job, but the past four years of working have been the most stressful time of my life. Even more so than the time I've spent raising my kids."

"Really?" I said, raising my eyebrows.

"Oh yeah, think about it. When a woman becomes pregnant, she instantly becomes a caregiver, nurturing the child inside of her womb for nine months. By the time the baby is born, the woman already has an established relationship with the infant. The child is an extension of the woman. When a patient comes in, they are injured or are in some type of danger. We have to get information out of them just to have some idea of who the person is and what led to the traumatic incident. A lot of the time, when it's bad enough, we have to resort to getting the information from the family members, and in many cases the family won't even show up or can't be reached. It's times like those that take their toll on your mental state." She finished changing my uncle's saline bag and then turned to me with a humble smile on her face.

I smiled back at her and said, "Why are you telling me all of this? That's a lot of personal information to be sharing with someone you barely know."

"Remember, Steve, I started the conversation, and besides I enjoy bragging about my job," she replied with both hands raised at her side.

Her confidence and humor became infectious and had me enamored. I directed my attention back to Uncle Avery after beginning to blush and immediately snapped out of my daze when I saw the increase of sweat on his body, seeping through his gown. I paused and recollected my thoughts, reminding myself why I was there.

"Brenda, is there any way we could get the air conditioner going in here? It's getting a little hot," I said, rubbing the side of my face with my right hand.

She glanced at Avery, taking notice of his appearance and said, "Oh, of course. Now that you mention it, it is a bit stuffy in here. I'll take care of that right away. Talk to you in a bit," and she walked out.

Checking my uncle's vitals and looking over him for a moment, I walked over to the window and opened the curtains to get some sunlight into the room. The view from the room was actually quite nice, overlooking the city and, of course, the parking lot below. I looked up toward the sky and noticed several helicopters distanced away from each other, hovering above the city.

"Must be an escapee," I told myself, not thinking much of it.

I walked back over to Avery and pulled a chair up next to his bedside. I rested my head back into the seat cushion, still pretty exhausted from the night before. I didn't get much sleep, and it had been like that for the past few nights. I was beginning to feel a bit stir crazy.

I could finally feel the cool air entering the room through the vents, and seeing that Avery was still in a deep comatose-like state, I closed my eyes and slowly drifted off.

* * * * *

Waking up to the sunlight hitting my face, I realized that the sun was setting as the darkness was slowly creeping in. I had been passed out for at least two hours. I got up from out of my chair and stretched my limbs, causing a few moments of light-headedness. I glanced over at Avery who was still lying peacefully in the hospital bed asleep. Poor guy; I didn't know when he would be awake from what seemed like an endless daze, but there was nothing I could do for him, and all any of us could do was patiently wait.

I peered out through the doorway, noticing the desk where the nurses and doctors sat but saw no one at their stations or anyone around that area. Then two nurses, not including Brenda, walked into the room.

"Mr. Williams, would you mind stepping out for a moment? We need to change your uncle's medicine bags and give him his sponge bath," the nurse said politely.

"Oh, yeah, no problem. I am getting a little hungry. I'll be back up in a few," I replied and walked out of the room.

As I passed the other rooms, I noticed that most of the doctors and nurses were occupied with their patients. I continued on.

Entering the waiting area outside the intensive care unit, I could see the other families calmly sitting and watching television, just some old rerun on TV Land. *Doesn't anybody watch the news anymore?* I thought to myself and continued walking toward the elevator.

I arrived, standing in front of the two metal-plated doors once again and pushed the button to go down this time. I casually glanced around at my surroundings and waited.

The bell rang, and the doors opened. I entered the elevator, only to find that I was the only one inside the brightly lit, confined space. Still feeling groggy from my long nap and gaining even more of an appetite, I suddenly realized that I didn't know where the dining lounge in this hospital was. I had never been to that section of the hospital before, only being here a couple other times prior. I didn't want to disturb anyone in intensive care, knowing that they were preoccupied with something much more important, so I pressed a random floor number and figured I could just find someone else to ask on another floor. Simple enough, I figured, and the elevator began to gradually move downward.

I arrived at the second floor and stepped out slowly, examining the hallways on each side of me, eventually deciding to venture to the right. As I continued walking, I couldn't find anyone around to help guide me, just one closed door after another on each side of me. I approached the end of the first hallway and saw that the only way to go was to the left. This corridor led to an exit just located on the opposite side of the hospital from where the parking lot and entrance were located.

"Great, just great," I said to myself as I turned around and proceeded back toward the elevator, hoping to find someone nearby.

As I ventured down the hallway to the left of the elevator exit, I could see that it was the same thing as before—not a soul in sight. Just more closed doors and corridors that led me deeper and deeper into the second floor. I began to sense trouble, noticing that there wasn't even an exit near—just long, vacant hallways, which became more and more disorienting.

I was starting to become a little worried at that point, realizing that I might be lost. I began calling out to see if anyone on the floor might be able to hear me. "Hello! Is anyone up here? I need some help! Anybody?" I yelled down the halls but got no response, nothing, just dead silence.

Becoming more and more concerned, I continued down the corridor, running in a panic. "Please, if anyone is up here, I think I may be lost," I said again and still nothing.

Just as I was about to turn around, I suddenly noticed something at the end of the hallway. I looked ahead anxiously, focusing my sight, not blinking once. My stomach began to turn as the realization of what I was looking at mentally blindsided me.

The gurney sat at the corner end of the opposite hallway on the other side of where I was standing. A cadaver was lying there with a white sheet draped over it. My hands instantly became clammy, and I froze in place. I called out one last time in hopes of finding someone: a doctor, nurse, hell, even a janitor would do.

"Hello?" My voice echoed, traveling down the hallway.

The sheet covering the body shifted as if it was a response to my call. My eyes never wandered from the gurney. The fear rendered me paralyzed. Catatonia had set in. I was unable to voice another word. Subconsciously, I was afraid that I had awakened the dead—a ridiculous notion indeed. The sheet couldn't have moved on its own. My eyes must have been playing tricks on me.

I continued to gaze ahead, surprisingly mesmerized at the sight of the corpse lying in the gurney. Similar to my fear of arachnids, I couldn't help but have a fascination with the eight-legged insects yet still repulsed.

The next thing that happened validated the fear I was trying so hard to suppress. The body began to slowly rise from the gurney, and the sheet began to gradually move its way downward, revealing a pale-skinned woman. She turned her upper torso to the right, toward me, making rigid, stiff movements, causing her to lean and fall onto the white, tiled floor. My instinct drove me to help the fallen woman, but my childish fear of death held me back, with the image of the covered body on the gurney still fresh in my mind.

Lying facedown, the woman pushed herself up onto her forearms and began swaying her body back and forth, crawling awkwardly, moving herself closer to the tee of the hallway. She extended her left arm, grabbing the lower left corner where the two hallways met. Her movements remained rigid as she struggled to pull herself up onto her knees. Once she managed to prop her upper half up, the white sheet fell from her body completely.

I took a few steps forward, pushing my fear to the side. It was obvious that this woman needed help, and I knew that I was the only person within the vicinity to be of any assistance.

The woman began to pull her entire body up, making it onto her feet but with not much ease. I could see that she was completely naked and appeared deathly ill.

My guess was that she was five feet, four inches, maybe one hundred and ten pounds and not at all intimidating. She had grayish blond hair, and her age could have ranged anywhere from midthirties to early forties; I was still having trouble discerning it.

Her skin was unbelievably pale, and her eyes seemed to have no life or color in them. They appeared to be glazed over in a milky white cloud, and as I slowly approached her, only fifteen feet away, I could hear what sounded like bones cracking with each step that she took. It seemed like she was having trouble walking, shuffling toward me.

As she got closer, she began making a horrible pained moaning sound, which her unfortunate condition obviously caused. Judging by her appearance, my guess was that she was experiencing the first stages of rigor mortis, but there was only one problem, she wasn't dead. With no hesitancy, my assumption went out the window like an unwanted tuna fish sandwich from the hospital cafeteria. Simultaneous to the strange guttural-like noises, she extended her arms out in front of her body, just beyond her torso, and began clawing out toward me with violent thrusting motions. Her jaws snapped sporadically as the cracking sound followed with the movement of her joints and other bones in her body beginning to wither.

"Ma'am, are you all right?" I asked her but got no response, just the painful moaning.

She was moving so slow as if her muscles and joints had stiffened, and all I kept noticing was how extremely pale she appeared—unusually pale as if she had no blood flow through her entire body. Not sure what to do, I just stood there in shock and looked on cautiously, waiting to see what her next move would be.

Snapping out of my daze, I realized that I had to help her somehow. I began unbuttoning my overshirt and quickly took it off. I ran up to the woman to cover her, but as soon as I was within reaching distance, she violently lunged at me and grabbed on to my T-shirt. I quickly wrapped the button up around her and brought the two sides of the piece of clothing together, covering her naked body. With both of my hands holding the shirt over her for just a brief moment, she then jerked her head downward and took a bite at my arm. I immediately pulled away from her and moved three steps back, but she just kept coming at me, seeming as if she had become rabid.

I briefly examined the wound and saw that it was not that bad; she had just barely broken the skin, but there was still a little blood loss. "Okay, lady, I'm just trying to help you. If you just calm down and come with me, I can try and find you some help," I said to her but still no coherent answer, just repeated biting motions and irregular body jerks.

She had pushed me back at least ten more feet before I saw a male nurse slowly come around the same corner. As he turned to face me completely, the first thing that I saw was a gushing wound on the right side of his neck, which had blood gushing out profusely. I noticed that he had also looked extremely pale, but, of course, with that amount of blood loss, it really didn't surprise me.

The two of these strange beings were both trudging toward me unrelentingly. It seemed as if they had caught sight of me on their radar and began zeroing in, with everything else surrounding them becoming nonexistent as if it wasn't even there. There was no real expression or emotion on their faces, and all I could see coming through their eyes was pain.

"Fuck this," I said out loud as I turned around and started running back toward the way I came from.

Halfway down the second hall, I turned my head around and saw their two shadows projected on the floor, still following me. The only noise that I could hear was my heavy breathing, my footsteps, and the god-awful moaning and inhuman groans which came from their direction. My footsteps were deafening in the absence of any other type of sound.

Quickly hurtling through the remainder of the long corridors, I had finally arrived at the exit which I had come across earlier. I plowed through the two large doors and began running alongside the wall of the hospital toward the front of the building where the parking lot was located.

As I ran out into the clearing, I immediately turned my attention to where my truck was parked, and suddenly out of the corner of my eye, I noticed a large object moving toward me. I turned my head over to the left and saw that it was an ambulance aimlessly barreling toward the hospital like a bat out of hell.

Grasping on to my bite wound tightly with my shaky right hand, I continued running toward the parking lot for my truck and ignored everything else happening around me. I reached into my pocket for my car keys and slammed into the side of the truck, stopping myself dead in my tracks. The force from the impact had caused me to drop the keys onto the asphalt beneath me. In a panic, I quickly picked them up off the cold, wet ground. I shoved the key into the keyhole, and as I began unlocking the door, I heard what sounded like screeching metal being driven through concrete. I turned my head and saw that the ambulance had driven halfway through the wall of the hospital. Orange light and smoke had emerged from the front end of the vehicle as the fire grew larger. At that same moment, about seven or eight of the hospital staff came rushing out the front entrances of the building appearing frightened. I could hear their loud, bloodcurdling screams above everything else.

I turned my attention away from the chaos and immediately jumped into the truck. I then jammed the key into the ignition and started the engine. Putting the gear into reverse, I pulled out of the parking spot quickly and proceeded to put the gear into drive. I took one more look at the destroyed wall of the building in front of me and finally got the hell out of there.

The Security Tower

Officer Ramon and Officer Sanchez scanned over the outdoor premises of the prison and the grass fields that surrounded the facility from the large security tower looming over the horizon—a maximum security penitentiary which held some of the state's most active criminals though small in its scope. Two major cellblocks are connected by an officer corridor placed just in between the two blocks. The administration and booking office were located at the front in a separate building.

Ramon stood at five feet, eight inches tall, with short black hair and a black goatee, weighing about two hundred and five pounds. Sanchez stood a bit shorter and a bit heavier, weighing almost two hundred and twenty-four pounds, standing at five feet, five inches tall and also with black hair—midlength—and a black goatee. Both men were Hispanic and could have easily passed off as brothers.

They shined the large spotlight, which sat next to them, in every direction on all sides. Other than what was illuminated in the fields by the bright light, all they could see was the tree line that surrounded and hung over the open grass and rose up to the dim city lights farther off in the distance.

"Man, I know we get paid a decent chunk for this shit, but this is fucking boring as hell," Ramon said to Sanchez as he continued to smoke his cigarette.

"You got that right, brother. Every night's the same…never any action," Sanchez replied.

"I'm hoping at least one of these dumb fucks tries to escape, that would for sure make my night, anything to get my gun off," Ramon said, and they both began laughing.

The two of them had been working together at the prison for the past three years, becoming close friends, going out for beers at the end of their shifts, even getting a chance to become familiarized with each other's families. It was almost comical how they practically became the clichéd stereotype of those buddy-buddy cop movies that had been popular at that time. They continued with their duty watching in silence. As both men gazed over the dark landscape, Sanchez spotted something moving off in the distance, just outside the field surrounding the prison fences.

"Hey, shine the light over there," Sanchez said as he pointed his finger northeast.

Ramon looked in the direction he had pointed to as he squinted his eyes, trying to make out what it was, but all he could see was very little blurred movement, making it difficult to identify what exactly it was that they were looking at.

After shining the light onto the foreign objects in motion for a few moment, the two men could see that the movement they had witnessed was coming from human beings, a group of people, about five or six.

"Looks like we got a couple drifters, must be here to speak out against the cut in visitation hours," said Ramon.

"Goddamn protesters," Sanchez muttered. The two men stood guard in silence, grasping their firearms tightly. They looked on as the group drew in closer, aimlessly stumbling toward the prison grounds and advancing on the fences.

"All right, go down there and tell them we ain't gonna deal with their shit tonight," Ramon said to Sanchez, nervously looking around, not sure what to do. He could sense that something was off.

"Fuck, man, what the hell do you want me to tell them? They've never come out this late," Sanchez said as he took three steps down the staircase.

The two of them stood and waited. Ramon kept his eyes locked. The group of unknowns approached the prison perimeter fence slowly, beginning to hone in closer. The three at the front of the group clenched on to the chain link and began shaking it violently, thrashing at it without any hesitation.

"Get off the fence!" Ramon shouted.

Sanchez ran down the stairway in a hurried panic. As he came storming out the entrance door of the security tower, he stopped himself, looking over the frenzied activity happening in front him.

"Go try and calm them down!" yelled Ramon from the top of the tower.

Sanchez cautiously stepped over toward the fencing where the mysterious group had collected, grasping his firearm even tighter, and as he inched in closer to the vagabonds, a dense rotten odor washed over him. "Oh, Jesus, what the fuck is that smell?" he said out loud. The noise and movement he had made seemed to have agitated the drifters as they began striking at the fence more forcefully, making loud, incoherent yelling noises.

"What the fuck is going on down there?" shouted Ramon.

"Don't worry, bro, I'm going to show these fuckers how we run things down here," Sanchez replied. He reentered the tower and went out through the second door, making his way onto the field outside the fence. The strange beings simultaneously began lumbering toward him, staggering in his direction. Sanchez started walking in a fast pace and pulled out his nightstick, swaying it back in fourth. "All right you, dumb fucks, you were warned and you didn't listen," he said with a grin on his face.

He quickly approached the member at the front and violently swung the weapon into his midsection. The force from the impact caused the man to be thrust forward, bringing him down to his knees. Sanchez then backhanded the man in the face with a close fist, knocking him down to the ground completely. He briefly looked down at him, laughing to himself with self-gratification and then turned his attention back toward the others. As he got a closer look at some of their faces, he noticed flesh peeling off as if it appeared to be rotting away. The smell intensified. Being caught off guard by the grisly sight, Sanchez paused and looked on in confusion and disgust. Before he could make another movement, two of the drifters appeared from nowhere, being within inches of him. They lunged toward Sanchez, clenching onto his arms and clothing, forcing him down to the ground.

"Ramon! Hey, Ramon! Help! They've got me pinned down!" he shouted at the top of his lungs.

As the remainder of the decaying beings began surrounding him, they drew in closer as he was lying there helplessly, struggling to break free from their strong grip. Ramon was already halfway down the security tower stairway by the time his partner had hit the ground. And just as he burst through the door at the base of the tower, the group had begun clawing and biting into Sanchez's face and body violently.

"Oh shit, get the fuck away from him!" yelled Ramon as he watched in complete shock and terror at what was occurring only ten feet away.

He began running toward his partner, but by the time he had made it over to where his friend was being attacked, it was too late—Sanchez was nearly halfway dead, the blood spurting out of the wounds and severed arteries. Watching on in catatonic state, Ramon gazed on as the attackers tore the flesh away from his cheek, simultaneously ripping the clothing away from his torso with their decayed, rotting hands.

They began biting into his abdomen, forcing through the skin with their yellowed teeth, violently pulling the muscle away and stretching the tendons until they snapped off completely from the rest of his midsection. Just before Sanchez began to lose consciousness, he began vomiting all over himself, brought on by shock and the horrendous smell that was coming off the bodies. He had already come to the realization that he was going to die. Ramon could smell the odor too; he had recognized the smell from before and remembered that it was similar to the stench of rotting meat, only much more pungent and nauseating. It had permeated into the open air.

He rushed over to where Sanchez was lying; his body was covered with the assailants who continued tearing him apart, feasting on his innards. His face had been halfway eaten, exposing his right eyeball. There was nothing surrounding it but muscle and the tendons that were still attached to his cheekbone and forehead. The skin had been completely torn away. The lower half of his face and neck were covered with the vomit and bile that he had regurgitated moments earlier. There was nothing Ramon could do though but look on as his friend was slowly devoured.

He rushed over to the group of cannibals, grabbed on to them one by one, and pulled them away from Sanchez's body with all the force he could muster. One of the attackers was able to grab a hold of the radio, which was clamped onto the shoulder loop on Ramon's uniform. The radio detached, and the assailant fell back into the grass. He could only pull three of them off the almost unrecognizable remains.

After being on the ground for a couple of moments, the attackers immediately began to rise up one by one, stumbling to their feet and shuffling toward Ramon. Blood and the chunks of flesh were now dripping down, hanging out of their mouths, the blood running steadily along their lower teeth and necks, covering most of the areas around their maws. Ramon pulled his gun out forcefully, yanking it from the holster and began firing bullets at the assailants sporadically. The bullets only hit parts of their bodies, mainly around the midsection. He noticed that the damage from the shots had no effect on the attackers whatsoever, just merely slowing them down. He aimed for their heads and began popping off more rounds. The gunshots rang out through surrounding area. The shots to the head seemed to have worked, bringing down five of them. There they fell instantly where they stood, hitting the ground after falling limp onto the grass field—no body movement, no nothing, just dead.

The other two attackers slowly got up from their knees, putting a halt on their feeding and began walking toward Ramon. He took a deep breath and aimed carefully. He fired off two more rounds. One bullet to the first assailant's head, dispersing blood and brain debris into the open air that surround them, and the second shot split the other man's skull right down the center. As the two bodies hit the ground almost side by side, most of the brain matter came pouring out from the back of their skull where the bullets had exited. A rush of blood, gushing out of the head wounds, followed the pieces of brain and skull, flowing with them. The blood formed into a stream that ran down the grassy hillside which resembled a river flow.

Ramon scanned his surroundings while wiping tears from his eyes. All that he could see were the lifeless bodies that were lying scattered, twelve feet in front of him. The bloodshed was unbearable, and the odor that arose off the bodies did nothing to help with the mad macabre. Seeing that there was no one else in sight that might be a threat, he began running back toward the security tower to trigger the emergency alarm and radio in what had just happened after losing his own.

Going through the tower entrance, he rushed up the stairwell, not letting anything slow him down. As soon as he reached the small cramped room at the top of the staircase, with his hand uncontrollably shaking, he frantically picked up the radio communicator which was connected to a transmitter unit. He called in to the inside of the prison. "Security tower to main post, this is Ramon. We have been attacked, I repeat, we have been attacked," he said, waiting for a reply.

"What happened out there? Has anyone been injured?" Officer Anderson said.

"Cannibals, about seven or eight of them. Sanchez is dead, he was eaten alive," Ramon said.

"Repeat that one more time," Anderson said in confusion.

"Sanchez is fucking dead. He's been partially devoured by about seven or eight attackers, cannibals. I got 'em, though, they're all dead," he replied while still in shock and disbelief.

"Sweet Jesus. Is there anyone else out there besides you?" Anderson said.

"Can you fucking understand me over this damn thing? I said I got all of them, everyone is dead!" he shouted, now becoming agitated with the voice at the other end of the radio.

"All right, we'll send some more men out there to check it out, just hold your position," the guard said calmly.

"Copy," Ramon replied.

He set the microphone down on the desk and looked up outside through the large windows of the security tower. Dismissing the alarm for the time being, he stepped out onto the walkway and shined the light down onto the corpses below. He could see the flies starting to gather around the bodies and couldn't help but start to feel nauseous, thinking of the larva being laid into the rotting flesh—nature was taking its course of action.

He moved the spotlight five feet to the right, over to where his dead friend was located, and immediately began to cry. The fact that he wasn't even recognizable anymore and his family wouldn't be able to give him an open casket at his service was just too much for him to comprehend; it was too soon after his passing. Ramon stood and looked on.

Keeping the light shined on Sanchez's remains for a few moments and wiping the remainder of tears from his eyes, he unexpectedly noticed that something was moving. An arm jerked up and then fell limp again. He peered in closer to try to make out what it was. It couldn't be what he thought. Sanchez was undoubtedly dead. But the next thing that happened shook Ramon to his core. Sanchez slowly brought himself to an upright position. Ramon could clearly see the exposed eyeball moving in the socket, looking up in his direction. The body slowly began to rise to its feet, and the remains of the innards came rushing out of the exposed midsection, hitting the grass. The blood that had collected inside the stomach cavity drained out from the large gaping wound and then continued to run down his pant legs. The body slowly began making its way toward the security tower, moving as if it was just beginning to learn how to walk—very similar to how a toddler looks when taking its first steps. The intestines, which were still attached to the inside of the torso, followed not far behind, being dragged through the grass.

Ramon was caught off guard and didn't know what to do at this point. The backup still hadn't arrived from inside the prison. He was out there on his own. "Sanchez! Sanchez! Can you hear me? Damn it!" he shouted.

Sanchez followed the question with a pained moan, barely able to vocalize any coherent response. Ramon ran back down the staircase and rushed through the entrance door, making his way back outside. Immediately, but cautiously, he jogged up to Sanchez and then stopped about two feet in front of him, still not knowing what to expect.

"Bro? Sanchez, are you with me, man?" he said in a soft tone. He approached the mutilated body, which continued to lumber forward. Ramon placed his hand on his shoulder. "Sanchez, it's Ramon, man, your best friend. Are you with me? They're sending us help right now. Sanchez?" he said as he studied the lifeless figure, examining the stomach cavity for a brief moment. Ramon was shocked to see that Sanchez could even stand up and maintain his posture.

There was nothing left inside the blackened stomach cavity. The bottom portions of his ribs were clearly visible. The attackers had devoured most of the major organs, and what was left of the intestines had been dragged through the grass field, spanning the distance of where he was lying before to where he stood. And then the attack came suddenly and without any warning.

Sanchez forcefully grabbed Ramon's arm, clutching onto it tightly. He dug his teeth deep into the tissue, on in through the muscle and tendons. His head jerked back, removing a fatty portion of blood-soaked meat that was taken from the forearm. Ramon fell, knees first, in agonizing pain and began feeling light-headed from the sudden amount of blood loss. He fell down backward onto the grass, barely able to keep himself upright. One of the last things he could see before slipping under was the disfigured body of his partner closing in on him, chewing on his raw, warm flesh with the blood dripping off the meat.

Sanchez's corpse reached out toward Ramon and kneeled down beside him, just before he went into shock from the intense pain. The horrible sound became obvious. The monster that was once a close friend of Ramon's had begun clawing and biting its way through the skin and muscle of his abdomen. Ramon caught one last glimpse of the attack through his half-opened eyelids as his life began to slowly slip away from him. The creature ripped through the flesh and muscle to his esophagus and all the major organs. It reached inside his stomach cavity with its hands clawed and began pulling the large intestine out, unraveling the organ as if on a spindle. He became dinner for his, once, best friend as the last labored breath left his body.

On The Road

I sped down the dark, desolate road with nothing but dimming streetlights to guide me through the black that enshrouded everything in front of me. I could feel my heart pounding through my chest, and my hands were shaking as I tried to retain a firm grasp on the steering wheel. The anxiety started to become overwhelming as the sweat poured down my face. I wasn't sure what had just happened back there. It replayed in my mind like a horrible nightmare. Those people at that hospital, something was terribly wrong with them, seeming as if they were brainwashed. The woman's contorted body was hardly able to move step to step. The discoloration of her skin and eyes. I could've sworn that she was nearly dead, if not certainly deceased. What the hell was going on?

I glanced down at the bite wound that I had sustained. The blood had stopped, but it had been throbbing since I had gotten onto the road. The areas around the teeth marks were becoming more and more red, beginning to swell, and it had seemed like the throbbing pain was slowly moving up my arm. "That fucking bitch," I said to myself, slamming my palm into the steering wheel.

Looking over at the passenger seat, I noticed that my work shirt was lying there. I reached over to grab it and delicately began wrapping the cloth around the arm with the bite wound, hoping it would numb out the area if tied tight enough.

I began taking deep breaths, trying to ease the anxiety away. It seemed to help a little, slowing my heartbeat down just a bit, but the slight feverish feeling remained. I rolled the driver-side window down to get some fresh air inside the cab of the truck and began taking it in through my lungs. After just a brief moment of having my eyes closed and letting the cool air hit my face, I turned my attention back toward the road.

SKRRRT! I had jerked the steering wheel over to the right as hard as I could while slamming on the breaks. The tires locked up and skid across the pavement road; smoke rose off them from the burning rubber. Something or someone was crossing my path, forcing me to act quickly. The sudden jerk of the steering wheel caused the truck to keel over on its side. The movement and momentum caused the vehicle to roll itself, still in motion.

On the inside everything within the cab was being thrown around me. The seat belt kept me in my seat, but my neck and head were being thrashed around from the violent jolts that the motion was causing. I could hear and feel each forceful impact that every side of the truck made with the ground. My head slammed into the door and the roof right where they met up for the door to close. The truck took one last roll before landing on its topside. The vehicle swayed back and forth for a few moments before it completely stopped. Smoke began seeping out from underneath the hood and slowly drifted off out into the open air.

I attempted turning my head to look around at my surroundings, trying to see where I was, but the whiplash had done its damage. I was almost certain I wasn't paralyzed though. My vision had become extremely blurred, and I could feel the blood dripping off from the side of my head. My eyelids became heavier with each passing second as I was having a hard time keeping them open. Blackness entered my vision, and I slowly slipped into unconsciousness.

Attempt to Maintain Order

"Fredericks, we've got a problem on the outside," Anderson said, running into cellblock B. Three other guards followed behind him, two of which were holding a gurney. A white sheet, soaked in blood from top to bottom, covered the body that was laying on it. Fredericks had requested that the bodies be brought to him after being notified of what had happened.

"Which officer is that?" Fredericks asked with a bewildered look on his face.

"Ramon. He was being fed on." Anderson stopped for a moment, taking a deep breath while wiping the sweat away from his brow. He continued, "By Sanchez. We had to take him down as soon as he noticed we were there."

"You mean…he was eating Ramon?" Frederick said. His face started to lose a bit of its color.

Anderson nodded his head. "He got up to his feet, and that's when we noticed the entrails hanging out from inside his torso. Strange thing is, Ramon told us over the radio that everyone was dead, guess he was mistaken."

"Sanchez attacked you?" Fredericks asked.

"He started coming at us. We tried to get through to him, but he just kept coming," Anderson responded. "It looked like he was going to attack, so we opened fire." The guard looked down at the ground, appearing confused.

"What is it?" Fredericks asked.

"It's just, he took several shots to the body, but that didn't stop him."

"What brought him down?"

"A shot to the head." Anderson slightly shook his head. The other guards could sense the fear and despair in his voice; the trembling in his breathing was so obvious. "I had never seen anything like it before."

Fredericks turned his attention to the gurney and raised the top left corner of the sheet to peer underneath at the corpse's remains. "Is he dead?" he asked, almost hesitant with his curiosity.

"You fucking see what's in front of you, right!" Anderson shouted, still finding himself in disbelief of what was happening. He swallowed hard and then said, "I apologize, it's just…there were more bodies out there. The smell coming off of them was unimaginable," he continued. "It's as if they had been out there rotting for days."

At that point, confusion had stricken the entire group.

"My guess is, they were vagabonds, drifters," one of the officers off to the side suggested.

"For now, get Ramon to the morgue," Fredericks ordered. "After that, go out and gather the rest of the bodies from the outside. We'll figure out what to do with them in the morning, but for now, we will keep them in the morgue. We don't need them stinking up the outside any more than they already have." He looked over at the two guards holding the gurney, making sure that they read his order clearly. They both just nodded. Fredericks turned to the third officer. "Got it?"

"Yeah, sure," the man responded with fear in his voice.

"All right, I'll take Ramon. You guys go out onto the grounds with as many gurneys as you think you may need," Anderson said. "I'll meet up with the three of you in the morgue, but if I'm not down there by the time you arrive, then come find me…make it quick." He took off one way, and the three other officers headed in the opposite direction.

Fredericks had other matters to deal with. He began making his way up to the second level of the cellblock, the tier which held Vincent Morris. Fredericks had gotten the idea in his head that Vince might have had something to do with the attacks that had occurred on the outside. Morris was known for working with gangs and other known criminals that had ran the city but only joining up with them and involving himself in illegal activity so that he could support himself. He was desperate, not having a job for some time and pretty much living on the street. Most of his family had passed, and the members whom were still alive wanted nothing to do with him.

On the night that he was arrested, Vince and the group he had been associated with at the time had broken into a house, which was a part of a wealthier neighborhood. The owner had been shot down in cold blood after trying to drive the men off his property. Vince's gun never went off that night, but he was there at the scene when the cops showed up, trying desperately to resuscitate the victim, but he couldn't save him—no one could have at that point. With all of the evidence pointing to Vince, the cops arrested him on the spot and took him in. He was later charged with murder and sentenced to life in prison.

Fredericks arrived in front of the nearly pitch-black cell; the entire row of cells to his right were in darkness. "Hey, shit-can, wake your ass up," he shouted.

Vince's lanky body was lifeless, no movement at all. He was just lying there in his bunk but had been awake since one of the guards had shouted "Lights out!" earlier on in the night. He had heard the conversation between the guards just moments before.

Fredericks began running his nightstick along the metal bars, waking up the other inmates as the clanging noise rang out through the entire block. "Morris, you hear me? Morr—goddamn it! Open up forty-two!" Fredericks said into his radio.

The bars slid open, immediately following the order. He rushed into the cell, grabbed Vince by the back of his jumpsuit collar, and pulled him off his bunk, forcing him to ground. He kneeled down, inching in closer to Vince. "So do you know something about these attacks? We know you've got friends on the outside, and if you're associated with the sick fucks that murdered two of our guys—my friends, then you're going to be in a world of hurt, Vince.

"Go to hell," Vince said, peering up at the guard.

"You, motherfucker!" Fredericks said as he raised his nightstick into the air, preparing to strike Vince. Before he could swing the weapon down completely, the door to the sally port slammed open.

The noise from the heavy steel slab echoed throughout the entire cellblock.

"What the hell is going on out there!" one of the other inmates shouted from his cell, disgruntled.

Fredericks rushed back out to the walkway to see what was happening. He looked down to the first floor and could see the silhouettes of two men slowly moving through the darkness of the cellblock corridor, but he couldn't make out who it was. *It's gotta be Anderson and the others,* Fredericks thought to himself. He hadn't seen them since they had left.

As the officer stood there on the walkway, Vince got up to his feet and bolted toward Fredericks, running the short distance. Coming up on him quick, he kneed him in the spine, which brought him down to the ground. Fredericks shouted at the top of his lungs as he took the fall. The entire cellblock erupted in noise from the inmates after being awakened from all the frenzied activity.

Vince grabbed his closed fist with his left hand and swung at the guard, hitting him in the face as hard as he could. The forceful blow immediately knocked him out cold. Vince looked over him to make sure he was unconscious as he removed the handcuffs from his belt. He then took Frederick's left wrist and cuffed him to the guardrail. In a hurry, Vince scanned over his body once more and noticed a gun in its holster, which was also attached to his belt. Fredericks, as well as the others, had armed themselves with firearms after learning of what had happened on the outside.

Vince unbuttoned the holster, moved the small strap to the side, and then took the gun. Paying no attention to the commotion taking place on the bottom tier, he made his way over to the stairwell and hurried down the steps. Once downstairs, he proceeded toward the prison cell control room at the front of the cellblock where another guard on duty was standing up from his chair, inside the room, to see where the noise was coming from. And then a dark figure appeared before him, moving cautiously toward the control room. It was Vince, slowly making his way from out of the shadows and into what little light illuminated from the small room. The next thing that the guard saw was the barrel of a pistol being pointed directly at his face.

Vince continued to advance slowly, keeping his eyes on the officer the entire time, never directing his attention elsewhere. "Open the door," he said to the guard as if he was giving him an order.

The officer pressed a button on the control panel that was simply labeled OPEN. The door slowly swung open, moving outward toward Vince. "Now get down on the floor, remove the handcuffs from your belt, and place them in front of you then slide your gun over to me," he said calmly as he walked through the doorway.

The guard slowly got down on his knees with his hands in the air, maintaining eye contact with Vince. He cautiously reached down for his firearm and removed it from the holster on his belt. He then slid the gun across the tiled floor toward Vince. The nervous guard proceeded to lie facedown. While looking across the floor at nothing else but Vince's feet approaching him, he reached down and grabbed the handcuffs from his belt. He moved the cuffs past his head and dropped them in place. Vince lowered his guard and brought the gun down to his side.

"Ugh!" the guard moaned in pain.

Vince's knee pressed down hard against his back, putting immense pressure along his spine. He picked the handcuffs up from off the floor while holding his pistol against the back of the guard's head. Vince grabbed his right arm and brought it down to his lower back, cuffing his wrist. He then got a hold of the guard's left arm and brought the limb down to cuff both wrists together, immobilizing him completely. He stood back up, scanned the room, and then peered down at the control panel to the right of him.

Something then unexpectedly came down onto Vince's shoulder. He jerked forward and quickly turned around. The hand reaching out to grab him belonged to a naked, paled body, appearing unusual in its appearance as it took each step with stiffened body movements. Vince raised the pistol up and pointed it at the strange man, lurching toward him. A constant guttural noise manifested itself from a deep place inside the man's chest cavity, sounding inhuman. The hair on the back of Vince's neck stood up from the disturbing sound and sight, causing goose bumps to emerge. He looked into its eyes and could see that the retinas were raised into the back of its head, sitting behind a white cloudiness that glazed over them.

"Stop!" Vince shouted, but the man continued to move slowly toward him, pushing him back further and further. He then realized that he had recognized the man from before, a fellow inmate. Vince had never associated himself with him but knew that he had been dead for almost four days.

The prisoner had suffered a severe heart attack in the cafeteria. From there, his body had been transferred to the prison morgue. "You're fucking dead!" Vince said quietly, confused by what he was witnessing. He impulsively fired off two shots at the man's chest, but the body continued to move ahead without any hesitation.

The other inmates began shouting, "What the fuck is happening? Who's out there? Who got shot?"

Vince looked at the man for several seconds and then fired off two more shots to his chest, making sure that he had hit the heart, but still the body would not go down. Vince's backside pressed against the wall at the back of the room—there was nowhere else to go. The gun was raised about six inches, and he shot the man in the head. Blood shot out, into the air, from the back end of the cranium. Bits and pieces of blood-soaked brain matter and skull splattered one of the windows at the front of the control room, the window which looked out into the cellblock. The body fell limp and collapsed onto the floor. The blood and chunks of brain slowly slid down the pane of glass as the fragments of bone followed.

The restrained guard on the floor turned his head to the right. The whites of two, lifeless, gelatin eyes looked his way. The blood from the body and head wound started to pool up around the corpse that was laying only a foot away from him. The red liquid began slithering downward in the direction of the helpless man, moving directly toward his face. Vince walked over to the doorway, glancing down at the corpse and the guard who was desperately trying to keep his head out of the blood, which continued to flow and collect around him. Vince stepped over the two bodies and looked back up.

Peering out into the cellblock with his eyes squinted for a moment, he finally began to see what was happening out in front of him after letting his eyes adjust to the dark. Vince immediately noticed a uniform. The shiny black shoes and metal badge reflected the light that was coming from the control room. There was a guard at one of the cells reaching his arms inward between the bars, desperately trying to get to the prisoner inside. He seemed to have completely ignored the gunshot and the fact that Vince had escaped from his cell.

Why doesn't he just order the cell to be open? Vince thought to himself and then yelled, "Hey!"

The guard was on the right side of the cellblock at the fifth cell closest to the control room. He slowly turned his head, backed his arms out from between the metal bars, and slowly began walking toward Vince.

"Who is that? Tell us what's happening," a voice from one of the other cells said out loud. All Vince could really see at this point was a black figure slowly stumbling in his direction. The sound of heavy moaning traveled through the large space which made up most of the block. The voices from the inmates seemed to have died down unexpectedly as they waited for some explanation, but Vince was lost in the situation as more thoughts rushed through his mind. *He should have charged me by now...I should be on the ground.*

The metal door at the opposite end of the block then slowly began opening. Five more bodies emerged from the doorway, one by one, but it was still too dark for Vince to make out who it was. The only noticeable features were the outlines of the bodies, a few moving more awkwardly than others, appearing as though they were limping.

He could hear the separate sets of feet dragging across the cold concrete floor. Bellowing noises emerged, almost morphing into angry yelling. The continual commotion riled up the inmates once again, and they began shouting in confusion, unable to do anything as they tried to get a look at what was happening outside their cells. The officer and the five bodies farther back behind, continued to advance toward Vince.

"What the hell is wrong with these guys?" he quietly whispered to himself. "Everybody, shut the fuck up!" Vince shouted at his fellow inmates. "Something's wrong."

The other inmates had no idea whose voice they were hearing. Knowing that Vince had escaped would only tempt the prisoners to get out themselves. At that point, Vince was not yet ready to deal with the ramifications that might come from that. He fell silent once more and withheld his identity for the time being. As bodies began to gradually get closer, Vince looked down at his gun, took a deep breath, and just stood in the doorway…waiting.

The Horrific Truth

"The number of attacks seems to be increasing by the minute. Although all evidence seems to be pointing toward a viral strain or some sort of disease, we have just received confirmation that the victims of these brutal attacks after being pronounced dead, and with absolutely no resuscitation attempts...are returning back to life. They are reported to be carrying out further attacks on living citizens. All over the world, the reports are coming in of these events occurring in different cities and villages. As shocking and delusional as all this may seem, it is becoming more and more clear that the bodies of the recently deceased are somehow becoming reactivated, focused primarily on one thing, attacking and killing live humans. Their motives at this time are unknown."

Click, the radio went silent as Vince switched it off. He sat on the floor at the back of the control room, resting against the aging white concrete wall. The radio rested on a filing cabinet right beside of where he was sitting. His initial reaction to the broadcast was disbelief, but it did not take long before it shifted into acceptance after realizing that he had just come face-to-face with the uprising phenomenon. There was no time to sit and ponder or have doubts and form questions whether this was a hoax or if the whole scenario had been concocted by some radio DJ, attempting to frighten the listening audience. Vince had been thrown into the horror headfirst before having any knowledge of the events occurring on the outside.

He got up to his feet, taking his time, being winded and a little shell shocked from the events that had taken place earlier. Walking over to the entranceway, he looked down at the guard who was lying motionless in the pool of blood with his head facing the opposite direction, away from him. Vince stopped beside the control panel.

He pushed down on the button labeled OPEN, and the door slowly began moving outward into the cellblock. The other inmates were conversing with each other in low monotone voices. Bodies were laid out, scattered across the floor in the cellblock corridor between the rows of jail cells. Most of them were lying facedown. Vince gazed out at the lifeless corpses and rested his left shoulder against the doorway, taking time to think to himself about what his next move should be.

"You got family?" Vince asked the guard after turning around to face in his direction.

The guard lifted the right side of his face up, out of the bloody mess, and moved his head to the right so that he could look Vince in the eye. "I have a wife, no kids. But my parents also live in town. You have to let me go, Vince. I have to make sure they're all right. I haven't spoken to my wife since I left my house this morning." Vince looked at the officer with a sympathetic expression on his face. "I've never disrespected or mistreated you or any of the inmates in anyway. You know I'm not like that," the guard said. "I have to know that she's okay, please, just uncuff me and you will never see me again. I will disappear," the guard continued as tears began to well up in his eyes and stream down his face.

Vince could easily sense how desperate the man was to get back to his family, and he had obviously been through quite a lot. Hell, he was lying in a pool of a dead man's blood, and Vince trusted this guard. He was right. He and the other prisoners never were subject to abuse and were never mistreated by the officer. A lot of the guards though; it was a different story. Most would wield their power as if they were playing god. The beatings were severe, and the verbal abuse only seemed to add insult to injury. But this guard would never partake in any of the mistreatment of the prisoners, even after being hazed a great deal by the other officers. He knew that the men were in there to be rehabilitated and, hopefully, have a second chance at life. To the officer, beating the shit out of the inmates was absolutely no way of getting through to them.

Vince glanced down at his feet for a brief moment, sighed through his nose, and then looked back up at the restrained man. "I'm going to let you go. Where are the keys to those cuffs?"

"On my belt, close to the buckle. You're going to have to turn me over to get them."

Vince made his way toward the officer, stepping over the stream of blood that ran between the corpse and the guard. He then kneeled down and grabbed the officer by his right shoulder, proceeding to slowly turn him onto his backside. The blood that he had been face-down in was seeped into his uniform from the back.

"Ugh," the guard cringed to himself as he felt the back of his shirt become sopping wet. The keys on the belt loop became exposed. Tiny shimmers of light tried desperately to reflect off the blood-covered set.

Vince unhooked the key ring from the belt loop and began flipping through each one. "Which key is it?" he asked.

"It's the smallest of the whole set, silver. It should be at either end," the officer replied and began motioning his head upward toward the key ring, trying to make it easier for Vince to spot.

"Got it," Vince said under his breath. He held the tiny key in between his thumb and index finger, leaving the others dangling from the large metal ring.

Once again grabbing the guard by the shoulder, he turned him onto his side, trying to avoid placing him down in the blood puddle for a second time. The key went into the cuffs, and the guard's arms were freed. He quickly rose up to his feet; Vince followed. Both men looked at each other, unsure of what the others next move would be. Vince had an alarmed expression on his face, worried that the officer would force him back into his cell, but that didn't happen.

Simultaneously the two men lowered their guard and began to relax. "I hope you find who you're looking for," Vince said and then raised the pistol to hand over to the officer. "Just be careful. The radio is making it sound like this thing is spreading like wildfire."

"I know, I heard the entire broadcast, and I will be, don't worry," the guard responded. He grabbed the gun and placed it back into its holster. The officer began making his way over to the doorway to exit out of the control room.

Faint beams of sunlight began creeping into the block through the small line of windows located closer to the top of the room.

Morning had arrived. "Vicks to control, do you copy? Evans, do you copy?"

Vince looked curiously at the guard. "That you?" he asked.

The officer turned around to face Vince. "Yeah, that's me, Thomas Evans." He proceeded to remove the radio receiver from his left shoulder loop, which was attached to his uniform. "This is Evan's, Vicks go ahead."

"Yeah, uh, we've got a problem out here on the outside of the perimeter fence.

"What?" Evans asked in a worried tone with a fearful look on his face.

"Garner and I are out here recovering the bodies that Ramon took down earlier and..."

"What? What is it?"

"Those drifters...there's more approaching, about forty yards out."

Evans and Vince immediately locked eyes. "Oh shit," Vince said, knowing that it must have been more of those creatures, and most likely, they were hungry.

"You've got to get back inside, both of you! It's not safe out there, not for either one of you," Evans warned the other officers who were holding their positions just outside of the perimeter fence.

"Bullshit, it's not safe out here. These guys are moving at an incredibly slow pace, and besides, there are only about two or three of them, not enough to pose any real danger. If they begin to give us any trouble, we will bring them down ourselves," Vicks responded.

"You idiot!" Evans shouted in anger. "You don't know what these things are capable of doing. Forget about the bodies for now, we will deal with that later. Just get back inside, damn it!" He stood by for a moment, waiting for a response and got nothing but silence. He had been cut off. "Shit, they turned off their receiver. They're not responding," Evans said to Vince as he turned to face him. Vince just stared off into nothingness, still in a state of disbelief. "I've got to get out there and get those guys back inside. Believe it or not, they're my friends, and I can't just leave them out there to die," the guard explained.

"So what are you going to do?" Vince asked. His sense of panic grew stronger.

Evans didn't answer; he was examining the weapons he had on him, making sure there were enough bullets in his pistol. He then looked down at his belt to be sure that he had extra sets of clips for the gun. He also had his nightstick with him. "All right, I'm making my way out onto the prison grounds to try and help those guys."

"Be careful out there," Vince said. "It may only be three or four of those things right now, but more may be coming. Try to be quiet once you're outside these walls. It obvious that whatever these things are, they are attracted to noise, so just have your guard up at all times."

"Don't have to remind me of that," Evans replied and quickly began making his way toward the exit which led out onto the grounds. He opened the heavy metal door, and bright rays of light from the sun poured in through the doorway, and for a brief moment the entire cellblock was illuminated. The light was so bright that Evans had to give his eyes a few moments to adjust. And like that the officer went out through the door, and he was gone. The heavy metal door closed behind him, and an echo from the large slab of steel rang out through the entire block.

Just like that the beautiful sunlight had vanished. The moans and groans of disappointed inmates emerged from different sections of the cellblock. The prisoners rarely had the opportunity to feel the warmth from the sun or even breathe in the fresh air from the outside. Evans opening that door was the closest they would get to enjoying nature—a drastic change from the cold, concrete, darkened rooms they were forced to dwell in day after day and night after night, but not for long.

Vince stayed behind, remaining in the control room. He was beginning to realize that it was for best to set his fellow inmates free, knowing that, most likely, the other men had friends or family on the outside. He walked over to the control panel that sat toward the front of the room. Second guessing himself for a moment, he ultimately decided that he couldn't be responsible for keeping the men caged up, having no knowledge of the walking nightmare which was occurring outside their walls. He took a deep breath and pushed the button labeled Main Cell Control. All at once, the cell doors slid open. From the first floor up to the second, the inmates had the opportunity to make their way out.

Cautiously a select few of the men on the bottom level of the block stepped out of their cells and glanced at each other with confusion. They then looked up toward the top tier at the inmates standing on the walkway, which ran parallel to each cell on the second level. The men up top curiously looked down at the inmates below. No matter how easy an escape seemed, though, all the men were still apprehensive about stepping out any further, in fear of being punished by the guards that had oppressed them for so long.

Vince made his way out of the control room and back into the cellblock. Faint sunlight slowly began creeping into the large darkened room through the small windows that lined themselves right above the jail cells on the one side of the cellblock. His footsteps rang out and echoed as the sound bounced off the concrete walls. "I'm sure all of you are wondering what's going on right now," he said out loud nervously. The trembling in his voice was undeniable. He repeatedly hit the palm of his right hand on top of his close-fisted left hand. Vince wasn't completely comfortable at that point. "And I don't know if any of you heard the radio broadcast from inside the control room that was airing a while back, but I'm certain you saw and heard the gunfire."

"Yeah, man, what the fuck was that all about?" an inmate to the left of Vince asked in a disgruntled tone. "You must have shot and killed over five people, including guards."

"Let me just explain. Like I said earlier, something strange is happening. I still can't really believe it myself." Vince painfully struggled with his own thoughts and words. He had never been great at public speaking especially in front of a group of prisoners.

"So get on with it, motherfucker! Tell us what the fuck is going on so we can stop worrying about the guards busting through here with their beanbag guns." The majority of the men collectively began shouting in agreement. Confusion and lack of information among the prisoners created an ugly tension that hung thick and low in the hot, musty air.

Vince looked down at his feet, taking notice of the damaged concrete floor and then let out a heavy sigh. "While I was in the control room cuffing a guard, I was attacked or interrupted by something forcefully grabbing me." The inmates fell silent and listened closely to what Vince was saying. "When I turned around and saw who it was, I was a bit caught off guard," he paused for a moment and then continued, "it was one of us."

"What the fuck you mean…one of us?" an unknown voice said from the large group, which began to pull closer in toward Vince.

"A prisoner…one of us," Vince replied.

"Who? How did he get out of his cell?"

Vince paused and then wiped several beads of sweat away from his chin with the tips of his middle and index finger. "In a body bag," he replied. The inmates looked at each other in confusion as if some kind of practical joke was being played on them. Vince proceeded to explain. "I know friends are few and far between in this place, but do any of you remember the man who had a heart attack in the cafeteria about four days ago?"

The room went quiet again but only for a few moments. "You mean Joey?" one of the inmates replied.

"What was that?" Vince attentively asked out loud, trying to find where in the large group the voice had come from.

"Herrera. Joseph Herrera. He was my cellmate and a good friend," the man informed Vince as he stepped out to make eye contact. He was African American, more advanced in his age and was sporting a shaved head. "He was a good man, and this place killed him," the unknown prisoner said while turning to look around at the other inmates surrounding him, being certain that they heard every word.

"I'm sorry. I can't be certain if he was truly alive or dead, but I had to take him out."

"Are you saying you killed Joey because you weren't sure if he was actually dead?" the prisoner asked. "He was walking around, breathing, you dumb son of a bitch!"

"I never said he was breathing, and you didn't see his eyes. Lifeless and pointed straight up into the back of his skull, and the smell coming off of his body...like rotting meat. On top of that, he was attacking me, biting at me," Vince tried to explain, but none of the other prisoners were buying his story.

"Bullshit," the outspoken inmate said in a calm but doubtful tone.

"His body is still in the control room." Vince pointed back but kept his body facing the other men, maintaining eye contact. "You can go in there and take a look for yourselves, and then you can tell me whether or not he was alive or dead before I shot him. Because I can assure you, a body would not smell of decomposition this soon after passing."

The group of inmates looked past Vince at the control room. The man, who once shared his cell with the fallen prisoner, began making his way through the group, carefully moving in between each body, alive and dead. Approaching Vince, a look of anger emerged on his face as the two men made direct eye contact. He continued to move ahead slowly toward the small room, passing right by Vince. Coming in closer to the doorway, the rancid stench of rotting flesh hit the inmate with force, permeating through his nostrils. He brought his forearm up to his mouth and nose, reacting naturally to the foul odor, and proceeded to observe the corpse. The pool of blood surrounding the body formed several different outward streams, nearly reaching the base of the doorway near his feet.

"You said he was up and walking when you shot him?" he asked Vince, appearing baffled by what he was looking at.

"Yes. Like I was going to tell you guys earlier, the radio broadcast was saying that the bodies of the recently deceased are coming back to life and walking around as if they had never died at all."

"And the bodies out there?" The inmate pointed to the bodies lying out in the cellblock.

"Same thing," Vince said, appearing just as surprised.

The other prisoners overheard their conversation, two of which began observing the dead bodies close by. One of the two prisoners immediately approached two of the corpses lying almost side by side.

They were guards. He looked back behind at Vince, making sure that he wasn't seen near the officer's bodies, but Vince was still conversing with the other prisoner with his back facing the other men. Hovering in place for just a moment, the inmate turned his attention back to the two fallen officers, proceeding to kneel next to them on one knee. His eyes quickly locked onto the pistols resting in their holsters. There was a set of handcuffs and keys still attached to their belts.

Fredericks, still cuffed to the guardrail on the second tier, began to wake up out of unconsciousness. Feeling groggy and nursing a pounding headache, he tried gathering himself enough to stand on his two feet, but halfway through his attempt to get up, he was abruptly jerked back down to the metal-grated walkway. The confused officer then realized that he was restrained.

"Shit," Fredericks said under his breath, looking over to his left and noticing that Vince was not in his cell. He then peered around at the other jail cells surrounding him and could see that they were also open and empty—no prisoners in sight. Suddenly a low murmuring sound emerged from below, now making itself present to Fredericks' ears. He turned his head to the right, peering past the walkway and down toward the first level, seeing all the inmates collected in the cellblock, casually standing around and conversing with each other in low monotone voices. Taken aback by the sight, he panned over to the control room to see if there were any other guards present but only saw the backside of an inmate—it was Vince. "Son of a bitch, he let this happen," Fredericks said to himself in a whispered tone. It then occurred to him that if the prisoners knew he was handcuffed to a guardrail, helpless—as he was—great harm would be brought upon him. Fredericks then became extremely fearful and quickly moved his head back and out of view, resting it against the walkway.

"We can't leave the other men wondering what the hell is going on in here or what's going on out there. This cellblock has become a community over the years, and we all trust each other for the most part. It's not good for those guys to question that trust," the man explained to Vince.

"I haven't made many friends in here," Vince responded in a playful tone, with a smirk on his face.

"Well, I never said all of us were friends," the man retorted, briefly raising his hands with his palms up. He chuckled.

Vince smiled, nodding his head in agreement and began to pace back and forth for a brief moment. He stopped in place and looked back up at his fellow inmate. "I think it's best that you tell them. I'm still fairly new in this block, and they wouldn't be so quick to disbelieve such a drastic notion coming from someone they have more respect for."

"Hey, man, I don't know nothin' about these guys having an ounce of respect for anything, just depends. You have a point though…I have been here longer."

One in front of the other, the two men walked out through the control room doorway and back into the cellblock. At that point, after waiting for about fifteen minutes, all the other prisoners had spread out among the bottom tier, many of them retreating back to their cells. It was obvious to Vince and the other inmate that the threat and danger of the current situation was not much of a concern to the others. Simply they had shrugged it off for the time being.

"Hey, fellas," the man said loudly, but no one acknowledged. He paused for a second and tried again. "Fellas, listen the fuck up!" he shouted this time with more intensity and conviction.

The majority of the large group stopped what they were doing and turned to the man, gradually moving back to where they had been before though a good number of the inmates remained in their cells, lying on their bunks, asleep. "For all you guys that have family and friends on the outs…they may be in danger," the man proclaimed. Immediately, there was dead silence. That one statement seemed to have grabbed the men's attention by the throat. "Now it seems that Vince here"—he turned to look at Vince—"that's your name, right?" Vince nodded, signaling a yes. "Well, it seems that Vince here was telling the God's honest truth. These people that have recently died are apparently getting up and walking again. Now I know that sounds like it may be a miracle of some kind, but the problem is these dead folks are going around and killing people, or so the radio says."

"So what? Were we supposed to be informed at some point about all of this? Is someone going to notify all of us about whether our families are safe or not?" one of the prisoners asked.

"At this point, if none of the COs have stormed in here to do a shakedown after seeing over the camera that we're out of our cells, with no guard on duty, then I'm assuming that most of them have either ditched their posts or are dead. So, I'm gonna have to say no," he replied.

Vince stepped forward to speak. "With that in mind, I think the best thing to do right now is try and make it off the grounds. Now is the best time for that. If the guards have in fact taken off or are trying to deal with whatever is going on out there, it must be pretty serious, and it's best for you guys with family or close friends to be with them right now." He paused for a moment and then continued. "For those of you without any loved ones, like me, you can hold up here. It's safe, and if we have to, we can try and go on a run for food and possibly weapons...*if* we have to."

The other inmates remained silent until one spoke up. "Turn on the radio. Let's see what they're saying right now about it," he suggested.

"Yeah, all right. I'll let you guys hear it for yourselves," Vince replied.

He turned, making his way back into the control room and grabbed the battery-powered radio. He quickly walked back out, raising the radio to about shoulder height and flicked the power switch on. The first noise that could be heard was static fuzz. Vince reached for the dial and began scrolling through the different stations, but it was the same thing on each one—broken up, static fuzz. He lowered his head in disappointment, but then snapping to, he slowly peered up at the wall behind him, just above the control room to the right.

"The TV. Let's turn it on to see if there's any reports coming in on the local news," he said with a nervous excitement.

Vince grabbed a chair from one of the cells and brought it out near the control room, just under the wall-mounted television.

"Someone grab me a nightstick from one of those bodies," he asked as he stood up on the chair. One of the other inmates brought the weapon over to Vince and handed it to him. "Thanks."

He extended his arm upward toward the TV and pushed the power switch on. The darkness on the screen was illuminated, but the only thing to be revealed were multicolored bars, which was accompanied by an ongoing alarm. Vince's eyes twitched frantically as he observed the screen. He moved the nightstick over a little to the left and began flipping through the other channels, but each station only served to present more emergency warnings.

"Well, all we get on here are the basic channels, and all those seem to be out," Vince said. "Though I'm sure the cable news broadcasts are still up and running, it's just we have no access to them." He continued to flip through each channel, in hopes of coming across anything that could be of some help.

Distracted, he was unaware that one of the other inmates was moving toward the control room up until he spoke out. "Fuck this, man, we should try to leave this place while we still have the chance."

Vince turned his head to the left and saw the man run into the room but did nothing. He just remained on the chair. The next thing that happened caught the other prisoners by surprise. The door at the opposite end of the cellblock, which lead out into the rec yard, slowly began to open. The inmate that had opened the door ran back out into the block, making his way toward the exit. Suddenly the noise levels went up within the group, and the others began to follow, heading straight for the same exit. Within a minute the entire block had been practically emptied. The men had made their choice while Vince had made his as well—he was going to stay.

Joseph's ex-cellmate, the man who had initially spoke to the group, also decided to stay behind. Vince stepped down off the chair and examined the corpses that he had taken out earlier, knowing then what to do. "What's your name?" Vince asked the man.

The man approached Vince and extended his hand out to him. "The name's Bernie," he answered, and they shook hands.

"Well, Bernie, would you be willing to help me gather all these bodies and store them into one of these cells? Just to get 'em out of the way."

"Yeah, no problem," Bernie replied. "The smell from that one body alone is starting to get a bit overwhelming. Can't imagine what this place will smell like once the others start to go sour. Keeping them all together in one spot may help."

They began to move the cadavers so that they could store them in the one cell that had been vacant for some time—the cell closest to the control room on the bottom tier. The process did not take very long, but Vince noticed something about the two dead officers while transferring their bodies. Both officers were missing their belts. He didn't think much of it. Most likely they needed to ditch them on the outside while trying to escape the oncoming attack from the creatures, or so he figured. Shrugging it off, the two men proceeded.

"I hope those guys don't get themselves killed trying to make a break for it. It would be a damn shame indeed," Bernie said to Vince. "No point worrying about it—just need to get this place secure."

After getting all the bodies moved, Vince and Bernie took a few moments to collect themselves and rest. The rest would be short-lived though as they both became edgy, not knowing what types of terrible things may take place within the next forty-eight hours. The only comforting thought to hold onto was that neither of them had anyone to worry about on the outside, and for that they were grateful.

"Gotta keep it secure, we've just got to for our own safety," Bernie repeated.

Vince kept silent in agreement, and from that point on, they were left to their own devices. Besides the other inmates who had remained behind to hide out in their cells and sleep, Vince and Bernie were completely alone and left with uncertainty.

Wrangling 'Em Up

It was late morning. The light from the sun illuminated the landscape below, revealing more of the oncoming threat that was headed for the prison. "It's getting pretty crowded out there, but I only see three...no, four guards. Two on the outside and two on the inside of the perimeter fence. Looks like they're trying to secure the area," a prisoner said as he looked on from the larger group, standing by, just behind the structured corner of the cellblock.

As growing numbers of the dead moved in closer to the two officers outside the fence, Officer Vicks drew his gun but did not fire, using it as a scare tactic to try to hold off what appeared to him as seemingly mindless beings, but that proved to be ineffective—they began to close in. A slight warm breeze blew through the grass field, which surrounded the facility, and the aroma of decay and decomposition swept over Vicks and his partner, Officer Garner, who was standing just a couple of feet behind.

"Forget about bringing the corpses back into the morgue, these fuckers are going to smother us!" Vicks yelled out as he motioned his partner to move back to the main prison gate entrance with his left hand, keeping the gun aimed and in continuous motion steadily from left to right in an attempt to hold off the oncoming bodies.

The smell of death and decay had alerted his instincts that something was seriously wrong with the situation, realizing that the roaming drifters might in fact be dead and could be a potential threat. Officer Garner paused for a moment to look on before running toward the main gate. Officer Vicks began steadily moving back but kept his focus on the rotting corpses moving inward, slowly toward him.

Garner, at that point, was at the main gated entrance, which led onto the prisoner transport pathway—an enclosed passage where new arrivals would be moved to the main front of the prison for classification and booking. He turned to look over his left shoulder and saw that Vicks was moving in a backward motion with his pistol still aimed at the strange beings who continued to move ahead and ease in closer.

Once Vicks had reached the entrance with his partner beside him, he motioned one of the two other officers inside the perimeter fence to go up into the security tower to engage the lock release for the gate. Immediately the responding officer quickly made his way up the staircase of the tower and arrived at the small station that sat at the top.

The roaming corpses were about five feet out in front of Vicks and Garner, but just as they were about to be reached by the creatures with their extending decayed limbs, the gate buzzed and gradually began to slide open.

"About fucking time, Jesus Christ!" Vick's shouted at the guard in the tower, frustrated by the lack of hustle. The two men rushed back into the prisoner transport pathway, where two large chain-link fences rose above them on each side, and with no hesitation, slammed the gate shut on their own. The lock engaged immediately, and the fence was sealed off yet again. They then made their way to the entrance of the rec yard. The tower buzzed them in, and Garner unlocked the gate of the reinforced electronic fence with his set of keys. The two passed through one after another. The guard in the tower scurried back down, and as he burst out of the exit door and into the yard, the other three men just stood by and watched as death drew in.

"All right, we should move now. The guards have their hands full with those things out there, and we've got to go while their attention is turned away before they decide to come back inside the prison," the inmate, nicknamed Gringo, suggested to his buddy, Carlos, and the rest of the group.

Carlos glanced over at the others for a brief moment, tightly gripping the pistol he had gotten ahold of inside the cellblock. In a brief moment of hesitancy, he ran his hand through his medium length, black hair and then replied, "Come on, let's go, Gringo."

Abruptly, with his gun raised, he began walking in the direction of the four officers standing by the perimeter fence at a fast but steady pace.

"What the hell are you doing!" Gringo shouted at Carlos in a whispered tone, but he didn't get a response. "Wait here, we're the only two with guns," he said to the others and then looked over toward the fence. He turned back to face the men. "We may not be back." And with that uncertainty being expressed, Gringo proceeded by following Carlos's lead, leaving the other prisoners behind close to the exterior of their cellblock, standing by and waiting for the perfect moment to move out into the open from behind the wall of the structure.

The dead, one after another, began to latch on to the fence, bringing the smell of rot with them. Their numbers began to rapidly increase. With curiosity Garner stepped forward a bit to get a better look at the ghouls then realizing how foul the smell was that was permeating off the bodies. He raised his white undershirt over his mouth and nose, which did nothing to help the nauseous feeling that began creeping over him.

"Garner, what the hell are you doing? Get back here!" Evans said in a stern voice.

"I just want to get a closer look at these things, see exactly what we're dealing with," he responded in a muttered voice and then took a couple more steps toward the fence. The fence began to move violently as the decaying bodies began thrashing away, being triggered by the scent of fresh, warm human flesh that had moved in closer. The metal clanging from the fence rang out. Startled, Garner jumped back in terror.

"I don't like this," Evans said under his breath. The other three remained silent. Then seemingly, all at once, the officers began to slowly move back farther from the fence, but all kept their attention on what was happening in front of them, and all being mesmerized by the sight of macabre.

"Hold it right there. Don't fucking move!" a voice shouted from behind the guards, loud enough to where they could hear the command over the moans and inhuman noises that the bodies were emitting through the fence.

Carlos stood in place with his pistol aimed at the four officers. Gringo held his position about eight feet to the left of Carlos, also with his firearm drawn at the men. Officer Vicks began to turn his head, attempting to see whose voice they had heard. "Don't you even fucking think about it! Keep your eyes facing forward and do not look at me. All I want you to do now is drop your guns on the ground, get down on your knees, and lie on your stomachs," Carlos ordered the officers in a harsh and infuriated tone. "And do it slowly, no games."

Officer Garner began to tremble, but he did as he was told and threw the pistol down, just in front of him, as did the two other guards. Officer Evans's gun was still being held in its holster.

"Do it now!" Carlos shouted.

"All right, all right, just let me grab it, and I'll do as you say," Evans replied, calm and collected. He slowly directed his right hand to the side of his waist, unbuttoned the small leather strap that held the gun in place with a single motion of his thumb, but paused before removing the pistol.

"Do it!" Carlos's patience was wearing thin. Gringo hadn't said a word.

In one quick instance, Evans pulled his gun from its holster and turned to fire but was not quick enough. A single bullet entered through his chest, piercing his left lung. He collapsed instantly to the ground and struggled to collect his breath. The barrel was still smoking when Gringo realized what he had just done. He froze in place, almost in a state of shock.

As blood started to pool up and fill Evans's lung, his attempts to take in oxygen only seemed to cause more problems. Violently he began coughing up blood, blood that he had then proceeded to choke on as it spewed out from his mouth and dribbled down his cheeks and chin. Breathing was no longer an option for the fallen officer as he began to slowly suffocate.

"Ah shit! What the fuck have you done!" Vicks yelled out hysterically, still unable to see the two men standing behind them.

"I said no games, but this fucker wanted to play, now he's going to die," Carlos said. "He's not going to make it. Put him out, Gringo."

Gringo's eyes shifted back and forth from the officers to Carlos as he hesitated for a second but then cautiously walked over to where Evans was lying. The blood covered the bottom portion of Evans's face completely and began seeping into his uniform. His eyelids twitched from the struggle and the asphyxiation he was experiencing. Gringo aimed the gun at Evans's head and then turned his face to look away. He squeezed the trigger, and it was over and done with.

"What the hell are they doing?" The group of prisoners all glanced down near the main entrance of the prison after hearing a single gunshot go off. They watched as Gringo backed away from the limp and lifeless body of one of the officers. He gradually lowered his pistol and took a few more steps back while Carlos held the other three men at gunpoint. With the barrel of his gun aimed at the remaining guards, the group of inmates stood by and waited. Carlos began to shout, nearly barking orders at the terrified COs, but from where they stood, the distance between the cellblock exterior and the perimeter fence made it difficult for the group to understand exactly what he was saying.

All three of the officers kneeled on their knees and proceeded to lie on their front sides, facedown. The group of inmates, near the exterior block, could then clearly see Carlos motioning Gringo over to the three men with his pistol. Gringo walked over to the officers and kneeled in between the two of them, removing the handcuffs from their belts. One at a time, Gringo cuffed the two men's hands behind their backs and finished his task off by doing the same to the third.

"All right, I'll grab their guns, you get the gun and cuffs from the dead one's belt," Carlos told Gringo. "It should be in one of his hands or somewhere near his body." He came in closer toward the restrained COs, where Gringo still stood motionless and dazed. Carlos kneeled in front of the guards to retrieve the weapons they had tossed to the ground just moments before. "Hey! Snap out of it, man. Those things are starting to collect at the gate. It's getting worse the longer we wait out here."

Gringo glanced at Carlos and blinked rapidly for a brief second, a reaction that signaled his return to the reality of the situation. He then proceeded to retain some motion in his paralyzing stillness, and was able to move fluently, allowing him to carry on with the task at hand.

Turning Evans's body slightly on its side, Gringo removed the handcuffs from the dead man's belt and began scoping for the handgun that Evans may or may not have dropped when hitting the ground after taking the shot to the lung. Gringo searched all around the body and found no sign of the weapon, but then glancing down at the corpse a little closer, he could see a glimmer emitting from Evans's lifeless, stiffened hands. The gun was still being held tightly in the dead officer's right-hand grip. Gringo rolled Evans's body onto its backside. He moved in closer and grabbed the pistol, attempting to pry the weapon from the dead man's unrelenting grasp but was met with a struggle to obtain it.

As each moment progressed, it became apparent that the undead on the outside of the fence were becoming more agitated with each noise and movement that Gringo and Carlos made. Gringo was starting to become impatient. Grabbing the gun, he took a hold of Evans's hand and began breaking each of the fingers that were firmly clenched onto the weapon. Slowly the officer's grip loosened more and more with each break. Gringo grabbed the gun by the handle and began moving the weapon back and forth slowly in an attempt to loosen the tight grip even more. This technique had worked as he was finally able to slide the gun out from the corpse's hand with much ease, and another firearm was at the prisoner's disposal.

"So what now, C? Head back inside and wait for all of this to blow over? Or should we try to get past these things and make a run for it, find somewhere safer?" Gringo asked with a nervous tremble in his voice. Without responding, Carlos turned toward the group of the other inmates still on standby near the cellblock, waiting for what seemed like hours by that point.

"Ha, ha, ha, safer than a prison?" Laughing the question off, Carlos looked at his cellmate as if he were a degenerate.

Gringo had no response as he certainly felt like one. Turning the serious question into his own personal joke, Carlos prided himself on making others feel so low to the point where they had to question themselves and their own motives. Nevertheless, the minutes were dwindling down, and it was only a matter of time before the undead dilapidated the entire west gate completely.

Carlos whistled loudly and raised his right hand as he began to wave down the band of prisoners. The inmates took notice of Carlos's call and, as heedful as they were, began to run across the flat, broad terrain. Crossing the emptied concrete basketball courts, the group slowed their pace and stopped as they reached Carlos and Gringo. A select few of the men were severely winded, having a difficult time catching their breath from the short run; one even grabbed his chest with his head almost between his legs.

"Now you guys who want to try and get out of here, good luck, especially to the fat fucks that can barely catch their breath." Carlos paused for a moment to ponder and then continued. "Honestly, if you stay here, you'll just end up slowing us down, so you're on your own out there because you're not welcome here anymore. As for the rest of you, if you want to hold up here at the home we've made for ourselves, you guys are welcome to stay," Carlos explained sternly and proceeded on. "Who here has family or friends they want to reach on the outs? Because we are only going to open that gate once."

"M-m-me, I do. I have my family I need to get to, my parents," one of the prisoners stuttered, still out of breath as he was shaking with fear. Going catatonic, the other men didn't say anything, afraid that they weren't safe from potentially being gunned down by any of the remaining officers that may still be on the grounds.

"Anyone else?" Carlos asked but got no responses. "So no one else, I'm assuming from the silence. Well, the three that can barely run six feet without having a heart attack are now acting as bait." Carlos proceeded to look over the group, spotting two guys he had been at odds with on the outside through gang rivalries but had since become allied with during his incarceration. "Gringo, give Jared and

Nathaniel guns and a set of cuffs. They're going to help us toss these three out."

Gringo approached the two men that Carlos had pointed out and handed them each a Beretta and a set of handcuffs. "Keep your weapons on them and keep 'em quiet. I have a plan," Carlos ordered.

As Gringo and the other two armed inmates violently shoved the three men toward the fence, which led into the prisoner transport area, Gringo suddenly stopped, taking notice of a pasty red colored object off in the field in the distance, just beyond the main road running parallel to the prison. "Hey, Carlos, do you see what I'm seeing?" Gringo asked, pointing outward as he kept his attention on the unknown red blur. His attention was drawn away from the expendable inmate.

Carlos peered through the chain-link fence, past the dead, to see what Gringo was talking about. The first thing that caught his eye was the faint cloud of smoke billowing upward and into the air. He followed the smoke cloud down to its source and immediately knew what the object was.

Writhing in an animalistic fury, the walking corpses repeatedly thrashed their limbs against the ever-weakening framework of the fence, trying desperately to grab a hold of the two helpless prisoners that had been forced to be exiled. In absolute fear and taken aback by the putrid rotting odor, they both tried pushing back in an attempt to further themselves away from the certain death that awaited them—only with no avail. The armed prisoners forcefully kept them in place, having a firm grasp on the backs of their collars with no let up on the energy which they were exerting.

"It's a truck," Carlos said, taking three steps forward, almost shuffling with his focus on the vehicle being unbreakable.

"Oh yeah, I think you're right, must have rolled over into that field not too long ago…still smoking from the hood," Gringo responded.

"Wha?" Carlos muttered as his attention turned to Gringo, only to see his dumbfounded cellmate had no restraint on the other prisoner who was on his knees with his head facing down. Carlos clenched his jaw and shook his head, lunging at Gringo in a fury.

"Man, get up to the fucking guard tower and open the gate when I say. Get your head out of your ass!" Carlos shoved Gringo out of the way and pulled the inmate up to his feet.

Gringo's forward momentum was halted only by colliding with the remainder of the prison group. Caught off guard, he looked up at the group with an apologetic expression on his face and then turned back to look over at Carlos, only to see him marching off toward the fence with the prisoner just in front of him. He turned back and quickly ran for the tower entrance. Gringo opened the door and passed through, tripping over himself as he scurried up the stairwell.

"When I signal Gringo to open the main gate, keep these guys in front of you for just a few moments for protection," said Carlos. "As soon as those things start moving our way, we let these three go. I'm sure they're gonna make a run for it. That should allow us just enough time and room to get through."

"And then what?" Jared asked.

"We haul our asses to that truck." Carlos pointed out the vehicle and then reached for his keys to open the chain-link door that led onto the prisoner transport pathway.

"I thought we were holding up here, now you want to leave?" Nathan said. "The thing is turned over."

Carlos looked at him with an irritated scowl and responded. "We're bringing those things in here. We're gonna need the truck to load them and get them back in. Won't be long before the fence folds, so we have got to go now."

"What do you mean we're bringing them in here? Are you fucking cra—"

Before Nathan could finish his sentence, Carlos suddenly drew his gun on him. "Don't fuck with me. We're losing time. We need to go now!"

Nathan raised both arms in surrender. "Whoa, whoa, man… it's cool. Like you said, we bring them in." Jared stood by with his pistol pressed against the back of the man's head, who was about to be thrown out. He watched to see what Carlos's next move would be as he prepared himself to come to his friend's aid, if need be. But after a moment, Carlos calmed himself down and lowered the firearm, redirecting it back at the inmate. He stuck the key into the lock and looked up at Gringo in the tower, giving him a head motion to release the electronic latch. Gringo raised his hand, acknowledging the signal. The buzzer went off for a second, and Carlos turned the key to open the door. He forced the unlucky detainee through the passageway and was followed by his two partners along with their captives.

They stood in place, gazing at the ghouls through the small openings in the chain link. The flies had followed and began to collect around the cadavers, frequently landing on the prisoners within the fence. In a final last-ditch effort, one of the three exiled prisoners pleaded for their lives. "Please, don't do this to us. You have to set us free."

Carlos drove the barrel of his gun into the thin layer of flesh on the lower back end of the man's skull. "I'm about to. Gringo, hit the lock!" he yelled at the top of his lungs.

Almost immediately, the entryway alarm buzzed once, and the gate slowly began to move from the left side to the right. The dead began to push inward. "Go now, go now. Force them back out!" Carlos bellowed frantically, being caught off guard by the rapid pace at which the living dead were pouring through the entrance of the prison.

The human shields proved effective, though, as Jared and Nathan pushed the men into the horde, enabling the corpses to snatch them up to be carried away for their feeding. Carlos followed not too far behind, letting his guy go to attempt an escape, with only three or four of the creatures tracking him. Without looking back Jared and Nathan continued with the plan and did not hesitate to make their way for the overturned truck.

Anguished, horrific screams were dispersed into the air. The two banished prisoners were no longer in view as the ghouls had formed separate groups around each man, gorging on their warm flesh with animalistic ferocity. At that point the majority of the corpses had been drawn and confined to the newfound dining area outside the prison fence, allowing for an opening and passage to the truck. Jared and Nathan crossed the main road, leading them onto the field located on the other side. Carlos brought up the rear and quickly caught up with the two.

A member from the group of prisoners, still on the grounds, snapped out of his stolid daze, taking notice of the cleared chain link. In a sudden realization, he knew that if they were going to make it out of the prison, they would have to go at that moment. He hollered up at Gringo, still in the security tower, remembering that he had the second set of keys. "Hey, man!" Gringo didn't respond at first. He kept his focus on the outside field, tracking Carlos, Jared, and Nathan. "Hey, asshole, down here!"

He finally took notice of the barking inmate below and stepped out onto the walkway, peering down at him, puzzled by his abrupt yelling. "What is it? What the fuck do you want?" Gringo asked in a quiet voice, trying not to attract any threats on the outside.

"Throw down your keys so we can get out of here," the man demanded. Gringo hesitated, doing a double take on the two hordes outside the fence, making sure that they had not been heard. "Come on, man, that's the whole reason we left the block. Outside of those two groups, they're pretty spread out. This could be the only chance we get."

There was no questioning in the man's logic. Gringo fumbled for the keys in his pocket and pulled the set out, proceeding to toss them down over the railing. The inmate caught the keys and did not say another word to Gringo. He turned away, bolted off, signaling the remaining inmates in the group to follow him with a motioned hand gesture as he began to run past them. The band of men hurried toward the same exit way, which Carlos had used minutes before. The prisoner at the front, leading the group, steadily slowed his pace as they approached the doorway leading to the main gate. The alarm buzzed once again. Gringo had disengaged the electronic lock when he saw that they had stopped. The man flipped through each key on the ring until finally coming across the one which would open the lock. He inserted the key, turned, and they were able to pass through.

As they approached the gate, the prisoner leading the group glanced over at the three others rushing for the truck. He noticed more of the creatures making their way inward from the opposite side of the capsized vehicle.

Gringo stood by, posted at the top of the tower as he watched over the fleeing men from inside the control room. He waited for the sign. "All right, as soon as we make it out, it's every man for himself," the prisoner with the keys told the others. "Gonna have to run until those things are cleared." The other inmates nodded in agreement. He turned to the tower and raised his left arm, waving it twice. The gate began to move, and one by one, the prisoners spilled out until the opening was large enough for all the men to exit at the same time. The keys were left behind inside the transport passage, and the men were gone.

"We've got more stiffs coming in just ahead of us," Carlos shouted to Jared and Nathan. "Shoot them in the knees to bring them down. We'll cuff 'em up to keep things safe. Kill the rest."

The three continued at a steady pace. As the dead came in closer, the men drew their guns. Nathan took the first shot, hitting one of the creatures in the kneecap. The body collapsed into the grass. The cadaver clawed at the ground, attempting to pull itself toward the approaching inmate. Nathan got down to his knees and grabbed the handcuffs from his shirt pocket. He struggled with the corpse at first before forcing the arms of the decaying body to its back. He brought the two wrists together, side by side, and proceeded to subdue the restless ghoul.

Carlos fired off a shot to the knee of one of the creatures but missed. The second shot made contact but did nothing to stop the monster. After the third shot hit but failed to incapacitate, Carlos became impatient. He rushed the cadaver and slammed into its body, knocking the thing down completely.

Before he could use his cuffs, Jared shouted in an alarming tone, "Behind you! One of those things fell out from the truck!"

Carlos turned around and noticed someone had collapsed from inside the cab, falling into the grass field. As the potential new threat began to stumble to its feet, Carlos calmly walked over to the vehicle. "Cuff that one up," he said to Jared, pointing behind at the corpse he had just taken down as he continued to just stroll along.

Unsure whether or not the individual from the vehicle had made the turn yet, Carlos approached the man, raised his gun, and with one quick swipe, struck him in the side of the head with the butt of the weapon, knocking him back down to the ground—the man slipped into unconsciousness. "Load 'em up!" Carlos ordered.

Wake-Up Call

The pounding sensation in my head had woken me up from the deep, unconscious slumber that I had been in for what only seemed to be a minute or two. It definitely felt like a severe migraine with the pain drilling itself deeper into my cranium. I placed the palm of my right hand across my forehead, trying anything to relieve the ache, but it did nothing to help. The cold sweats suddenly came on, nearly soaking the T-shirt I was wearing. The feeling was similar to that of having the flu, shifting back and forth from cold to hot within a matter of seconds. The bones in my body felt like glass, aching from what could only be described as a slow deterioration of calcium.

With my palm still rested over my head, I noticed that the veins running across my forearm were discolored, having turned into a darkened purple hue. My eyes wandered from my inner wrist and upward until seeing the piece of cloth that was secured around my arm, just before the base of the joint. Blood had seeped through the fabric, making its way to the surface. I grasped onto the torn shirt and gently slid it downward, revealing the bite marks that I had received from the woman at the hospital. The blood in the teeth indentations had dried, turning into blackened scabs; they appeared to be infected. My entire right arm continued to throb in pain. There seemed to be a correlation between the headache and the twinge in my arm, almost as if working off one another. I reached down to run my fingers across the bite but immediately withdrew, realizing that the tenderness of the wound was far too severe.

The sudden sting of nerves had my eyes wide open as I began to process where I was—a small concrete room maybe a little larger than an average-sized bathroom. Two beds in the form of bunks and a singular toilet/sink combination, which my upper body was resting against when I had come out of unconsciousness, sitting on the ground upright—this was a prison cell.

I tried to remember how I may have ended up here, but all I could recall was fleeing the hospital and flipping my truck. The whole situation didn't make any sense, and the grogginess and confusion only seemed to add to my headache. I should have woken up in a hospital bed, but after my prior situation, the cold, prison cell floor would have to do.

I closed my eyelids and rubbed them for a brief moment to rid the sleep away before propping my arms up to get to my feet. A faint panting noise made itself evident as I peered through the metal bars just across from me. A uniformed officer sat in a wooden desk chair, bound, with his hands cuffed behind his back and a strip of duct tape secured around his mouth and neck, sealing off the guard's lips. His attention was focused over to his right at the other cells beside mine. I don't even think he was aware that I was present. I could see endless beads of sweat pouring down his face and noticed an uncontrollable twitch in his fear-stricken eyes as he hopelessly tried to free his hands through the tightly fastened cuffs around his wrists.

I took in a deep breath, attempting to speak to the man, but my mind went blank as I was truly at a loss for words. Before I could even gather my thoughts or try to process what I was seeing, a stern voice emerged from one end of the block, to the left of me, interrupting my attempted concentration. I got back on the ground cautiously and quietly pulled myself across the cold, stone floor to the foot of the bottom bunk. The guard caught notice of my movement and looked down at me, shaking his head as if he was signaling me to remain low-key, obviously worried that I would attract attention. Our eyes locked, and we both became motionless and silenced. I listened closely, hoping that my questions would soon become answered, but the officer already seemed to have an idea of what was taking place.

"Sure, I've taken lives before, and that's what got me in here. I'm not dodging guilt because frankly I don't have any. But you, the men and women that work for this prison, have taken something that isn't even yours to touch, the choice of people that aren't in here, innocent people, our families. You robbed both sides by keeping us stowed away and hidden 24-7, driving them off at the front gates and destroying any chances for visitations or contact. With all that has been going on in the past couple of hours, you must be worried about your families on the outside, vulnerable to this threat, but that's a waste of energy because they are probably already dead…as with mine. Everyone outside these walls is weak."

Now I was starting to become panicked as I felt my stomach drop down to the pit. I had only been awake for five minutes and was being held in a dingy, prison cell for reasons I didn't know. A restrained guard sat just outside the bars in front of me. Someone's plan was coming to fruition quickly. I leaned over as far as I could to my right in hopes of catching a glimpse of the man spewing his monologue, but he was too far out of my sight to get a good look. Scoping the surrounding block, my first inclination was that he was an escaped inmate. The majority of the cells, at least within my sight, were empty, with the exception of a few men either napping on their bunks or pacing back and forth inside their tiny, cramped rooms.

As a precaution, I rolled to my bottom side and began to drag myself back away from the bunk and metal bars. It didn't take me long to reach the opposite wall, where I had woken up just moments earlier, near that disgusting toilet. I remained in the shadows, hoping no one else would see me, and I knew the guard wouldn't give me away; he was obviously concerned about his own ass. His fear seemed to increase significantly as the rant from the unknown man continued, only becoming less audible to my ears but still, undoubtedly, causing me alarm.

Was I being held in this cell to eventually be killed off? Questioning the outcome of my own life, I suddenly thought of my sister, Claire. She was the last important person whom I had in my life, and I didn't even know if I was ever going to see or talk to her again. Tears began welling up in my eyes, but I forced them back and wiped them away, knowing that if there was some chance of survival, I would need to focus. I continued to listen in on what the man was saying.

"Inside of these cells, the walking corpses of once living human beings are being held. We brought them into our house to show you what they do, and you will experience that firsthand. Once those doors open, you will be forced in there and you will attempt to fight for your lives. We are going to feed you to these things, and nothing you say or do is going to change that. You will face the repercussions of the pain and agony you caused us and our families within the past two years. Most likely you will be eaten alive, and in time you will come back as one of these creatures. At that point my men and I will shoot all of you in the head, finishing our job. Balance will be restored."

I could hear the other restrained guards begin to thrash their chairs around. I assumed that they were trying to free themselves from the handcuffs around their wrists and the duct tape strapped around their ankles. Muffled groans emerged as the chairs continued to hobble around. The wood bounced on the concrete floor, producing loud, echoing noises throughout the block. The officers were trying to call for help, but there was no one around to be of any assistance. At that point, all that I could hear from the armed inmate was a mocking laughter at their desperate attempts to escape.

"A piece of advice, all that noise isn't gonna do you any good. It only serves to rile up whatever those things are. If I were you, I would calm myself and keep quiet. You don't want to be thrown into a cell when they're rabid. At least give yourselves a fighting chance. If you shut the fuck up, this will go by quick and easy," the armed prisoner informed the guards and then a moment of brief silence before the sound of shallow panting and weeping made its way down to my cell.

The officer that sat in front of me had his head hung low, obviously realizing the undeniable defeat. It was a sad and strange thing to observe a man who was going to face certain death just sitting there having given up, but as far as my fate was concerned, I truly did not know which was all the more terrifying.

Feeding The Undead

"Nathan, help me get him to his feet," Carlos ordered.

Nathan stood just off to the right of Carlos, by himself. Jared had been bit while trying to subdue the corpse that Carlos had taken down earlier that afternoon. Seen more as a weak link rather than a threat, potentially compromising the operation that had been planned, Carlos shot him dead and left his body out in the grass field. Gringo remained behind Carlos and Nathan, withdrawn from the actions taking place. Carlos grabbed ahold of Officer Garner's upper left arm and Nathan followed, grabbing his right. The two lifted the officer up, out of the wooden chair, and kept him standing in place with his hands cuffed behind his back and a strip of tape over his mouth.

The creature inside the cell dragged itself across the floor, periodically letting out a deep, guttural moan as it moved within the small space. Carlos reached for his set of keys and freed Garner from the uncomfortable restraint. He proceeded by removing the duct tape, which was beginning to lose its hold and peel back from the copious amounts of sweat pouring out from his face. Garner did not make any attempt to break loose or escape; there was no point, he had decided, and just glared into Carlos's eyes with a look of disdain.

"Open cell four," Nathan said to Gringo. He didn't respond or even acknowledge the order. Nathan looked back at him for a moment and then turned to Carlos, shrugging his shoulders and shaking his head.

"Gringo, open the fucking cell!" Carlos shouted.

Gringo flinched at the sound of his voice like a scared puppy. He immediately sauntered over to the control room, and a second later, the cell gate began to open.

Carlos punched Garner in the stomach with brutal force, and he collapsed to his knees. Nathan kicked the guard from behind, forcing him into the cell. He fell face-first onto his front side. The bars closed behind him. Streaks of blackened blood trailed close behind the debilitated ghoul, gushing from the gunshot wounds which it had sustained after being shot through the kneecaps. The creature swayed from side to side, pulling itself closer to Garner without any hesitation. Bernie and Vincent hung back in an open cell, observing everything unfold before them but reluctant to stop the execution. They did and said nothing.

Garner peered up at the crawling cadaver and said under his breath, "What the fuck?" immediately inhaling the foul stench that permeated through the cell. He fidgeted his body and tried to distance himself from the corpse as far back as possible. The limited amount of space only allowed for him to move about fifteen inches to the base of the cell bars. He was able to get up to his knees, resting his chest and face against the bars. From behind Garner felt a hand palm the top of his skull. Nails dug into the skin on his forehead just below the hairline. Blood began to trickle down his face.

"Oh shit, Nathan, someone must be hungry," Carlos said and began laughing.

Nathan hesitantly snickered with a smile and quietly replied, "Yeah, must be." As with many of the others, he was having trouble adapting to the notion that these people, these things, were in fact dead.

The creature clenched onto Garner's left shoulder and raised itself up, creeping over his backside. Sensing the fresh blood, it ravenously bit into the open wounds and began pulling back on the scalp to release the flesh from the bone. Garner screamed in agony, and the chilling sound rang out through the cellblock. The blood began pooling up in the shallow space where the skull had been exposed. His body was pulled back to the ground from the strength put forth by the horrific being. The skin being torn away sounded like a bedsheet being ripped apart as the fibers were being separated. The red fluid spilled over onto the concrete floor, forming an ever-growing puddle for the undead body to bathe itself in.

Many of the other inmates who were holding up in their cells, some napping, were awakened and brought out by the echoing cries of the dying guard. From their vantage point, the only things discernible inside the cell were two bodies on the floor. One in a CO uniform, lying limp and lifeless, surrounded with blood and the other, violently active, clawing into the facial tissue, consuming the flesh to the point where no meat remained. Only two naked eyeballs and exposed bloodstained teeth were visible. A handful of the prisoners cheered and applauded the grisly sight.

"Death to the swine!" one man shouted.

Several others followed with the chant. "Death to swine, death to swine!" The remainder of the men said nothing and retreated back to their cells.

Vince stood up and took a few steps forward. Bernie jumped to his feet, grabbed his arm, and stopped him. "What the hell are you doing, man? You can't go out there."

"No one else is doing anything. I've got to say something, or he's going to kill the other guards and eventually the rest of us," Vince replied.

Bernie paused for a moment and let out a heavy sigh. "Vince, if you do that, you're only going to piss him off even more, and they'll kill you anyway. I mean look at it out there."

Vince peered through the spaces between the bars and off to the right. "What's your point?"

"My point is that he's got two other guys working with him that are armed, plus he has a gun not to mention the other inmates just waiting to rally behind him," Bernie said. Vince clenched his teeth and gently punched the wall beside him, frustrated that he couldn't act on the situation. He turned around, walked past Bernie, and sat back down on the lower bunk.

Officer Vicks sat in front of the cell next to Garner's, on the left-hand side, with his hands bound together. Carlos casually strolled over and stood behind him. Two arms from within the cell extended out through the bars, toward the guard, only inches away from his face. The creature was standing upright and was more than capable of walking, being unaffected by the gunshot wounds that it had received earlier—the same creature that had bitten Jared.

"All right, same as before," Carlos said, and he motioned his head for Nathan to come over. Carlos, once again, grabbed onto the second officer's left arm.

Before Nathan could even take a step, he caught something moving out of the corner of his eye. He turned around and saw Vince walking over toward them. "Yo, Carlos, we've got a visitor."

Carlos turned and saw the inmate trudging over. "What? Did you want a front row seat to the show? 'Cause there are plenty of openings," he said to Vince with his arms raised in question. Vince did not respond and continued moving. Carlos reached for his pistol and aimed, stopping him dead in his tracks. "You better speak, Vince, or you're gonna be joining the open buffet."

"Look, I get why you're doing this, but killing these men isn't going to change or bring back the time you've lost with your family. You know these guys were just following orders from the warden. He's the true enemy in all of this," Vince explained.

"Come on, Carlos, don't listen to this wannabe gangster. You and I both know that all of the COs and the warden enjoyed watching us suffer," Nathan said.

"Both of you, just shut the fuck up. Vince, if you're so eager to suck these guys off, then maybe you should be strapped into one of these chairs along with them. Like I said, we've got plenty of openings."

"Fine, Carlos, I'll comply, but at least let Fredericks go free. He is only here because of me. I was the one who cuffed him to the railing. You don't have to kill him," Vince said, pleading with the prisoner.

"Oh, you mean that piece of shit sitting in front of cell seven? Well, why don't we bring him over here to switch places with Vicks? He'll get a head start." Carlos threatened.

"All right, all right, you win, Carlos. I will go back to my cell. Just leave Fredericks where he's at for right now," Vince said desperately.

"Sounds fair enough, we got a deal. Just get the fuck out of here…and if you interfere again, I'll shoot you myself," Carlos said.

Vince had no other choice but to retreat. He was unarmed and had no means to defend himself. He made his way back to his room where Bernie still sat calmly. He looked up at Vince and said, "What did I tell you, man? That was a pointless and stupid. You better just hang back from here on out, no matter how many people in here may die."

"Gringo, get out there and make sure Vince and the others stay in their cells," Carlos ordered.

Gringo stood in the doorway of the control room and paused as he stared at the floor, avoiding eye contact with Nathan and Carlos. "Sure, but can I ask you why I'm playing babysitter all of the sudden?"

Carlos laughed in shock, as if the question could answer itself, and then responded, "Well, for the past couple of hours, you haven't done much but open and close doors." He looked over the entire block and continued. "Now that shit has hit the fan, this world has shown me your true colors."

"Oh yeah, Carlos, and what's that?" Gringo immediately fired back.

"You're a little bitch, and if you were out there on your own or didn't have protection in here, I guarantee you that you would be dead by now. I was convinced I had changed you. I taught you how to fight and to stand up for yourself in this shit hole, but it looks like it was just a waste of time. You're still just a withered, weak little white boy."

Gringo shook his head and bit his tongue. He wasn't going to waste one more second arguing. "I've got my gun. Are we done here so that I can start my rounds?" Carlos didn't say anything. "Good," Gringo said as he turned his back and began walking in the opposite direction from Nathan and Carlos.

He had made a couple of rounds through the block before approaching Vince and Bernie's cell. "What the fuck do you want? Come to make sure we don't disrupt Carlos's plans?" Vince asked in a disgruntled tone.

"No...actually the opposite. I want to help you take Carlos and Nathan down before they kill anyone else," Gringo said and reached down for his firearm. "Here, take my gun. I want you to hold onto it...and when the opportunity presents itself...we act.

"And what motivated you to just all of the sudden switch sides?" Vince said.

"I'm sick and tired of taking orders and being intimidated by that piece of shit. He needs to be taken out," Gringo responded.

"I don't know how easy that's going to be. Carlos has Nathan and, potentially, several other prisoners who have his back," Vince pointed out.

"Nathan, after all the other guards have been killed off, we are going to take out the rest of the remaining inmates. They have become too much of a risk to keep around, especially after seeing what Vince was willing to do. It's not going to work keeping them around," Carlos said.

"I don't know, Carlos, I don't really see any of the others being a threat to us. We should just leave them be. We may need their help later on," Nathan said.

"Oh, is that how you feel, Nathan? Maybe I should just kill you," Carlos responded in calm but angered tone. He paced around in a circle and then raised his gun, firing off one shot to Nathan's chest. Carlos walked over to the wounded man who had fallen onto his knees. He desperately clawed at his own chest in panic, with some hope of removing the slug from the damaged tissue but with no avail.

Carlos grabbed Nathan's collar and proceeded to drag him over to the cell where Vicks sat. "You, son of a bitch," Nathan said with a struggle as he began to cough up and choke on his own blood.

Carlos pushed Vicks off to the side with his foot and planted Nathan in front of the prison cell. "You're not with me, then you're against me!" Carlos shouted.

He rushed over to the control room and opened the cell door. Nathan collapsed onto his side and began spitting up blood, not long before passing out. The ghoul inside the chamber immediately sensed the fresh blood and grabbed onto the dying man, pulling him inside with one violent motion. Carlos watched in awe and without closing the cell, walked over closer to witness the feeding. He wasn't taken aback by the gore at all…he was getting off on it.

"Hey, Gringo, get your ass back over here and close cell nineteen!" Carlos yelled out, keeping his attention on the feeding of Nathan's mutilated carcass and the reanimated corpse which proceeded to gorge itself on the flesh. He got no response. "Yo, did you hea—" Carlos turned around and saw Vince standing there with Gringo's gun aimed right between his eyes.

Bernie stood just a couple of feet behind Vince with Gringo standing even farther back, inherently ashamed by his deceit, but nonetheless he had Vincent's back. Carlos smiled and laughed to himself with his eyes closed.

He sighed with the fading laughter and said, "You've gotta be fucking kidding me."

The Warden

Warden Unitas stood idly by in his office near the large window, with the blinds cracked just enough for him to peer out into the open prison grounds below. He continued to wedge his right thumbnail in between his upper and lower front teeth, witnessing the undead creatures collecting outside the perimeter fence. His glasses gradually slid down the bridge of his nose from the beads of sweat beginning to form on his face.

For the prisoners, he came off as a power-hungry, egotistical monster, but once the real threat of humans feeding on other humans had emerged, Warden Unitas was reduced into a timid coward, unable to run his own facility. Communications had failed quickly between the National Guard, the federal state government and even the state police. Contact with many of his own correctional officers had been diminished. The loss of control terrified Warden Unitas more so than the cannibalistic monsters wandering inside his walls and outside the gates.

And then a sudden knock on the door. "Warden Unitas, it's Officer Wells, you need to let me in." Susan Wells was one out of a handful of guards who had survived and one of the few female officers working for the penitentiary.

With a trembling hand, the warden opened the door, and the stocky, blond CO stormed into the office, past the sheepish-looking leader in command. Warden Unitas closed the door and casually walked back over to the same window which he was looking through before. He resumed gazing outside. The sky was partially overcast, but the chance of rain was unlikely.

"Sir, I'm not sure if you know what's going on out there, but no one has been able to reach any of the other COs from cellblock B. Block A is secure, but we think there might have been a breach in B," Wells said.

The warden did not respond. Susan stared at his backside in disdain, waiting for a response, but it seemed that he was in a daze, lost in the vision he had of what the world was becoming.

"Sir, it's highly likely that several of your inmates have made it off of the grounds, and you've been nowhere to be seen. You're not even answering your phone."

"Oh, I know they did," the warden said in a faint but confident tone of voice.

"What did you say?" Susan asked.

"The group of prisoners from block B that you believe escaped... they did earlier today around noon." He looked over his shoulder at Susan and could see the bewildered look on her face. She stood speechless. "They shot and killed one of our guards. Things got out of control. What was I supposed to do?" the warden explained, facing Officer Wells.

"What happened to the two other officers?" Susan asked calmly.

"Three inmates took them captive, brought them back in along with those cannibals. My god, I can smell them from here, putrid." The window was slightly cracked open.

"How did they get that many bodies inside? The majority of them are outside of the fences."

"With a truck. Three or four other prisoners made it outside of the fences and found a truck turned over on its topside out in the grass field. They took down a couple of the assailants and flipped the truck back onto its wheels," the warden explained.

"If you saw them come back in, then that means they're most likely back in cellblock B...and now they have hostages," Susan said anxiously and began pacing back and forth.

Warden Unitas cleared his throat and said, "Yes, I suppose."

Susan stopped herself and turned to speak. "Why the hell didn't you do anything? Several of those men down there are extremely dangerous, murderers, rapists. There's a good chance those guards are dead by now."

"You may be right, but that doesn't mean we risk anymore lives trying to save them, especially when they're most likely dead," the warden said.

"But there still might be a chance that they are alive. The prisoners may be using them as leverage."

"Well, beside that point, I still think it's too dangerous to risk our lives in an attempt to rescue officers that are more than likely dead, and we know for a fact that the inmates are concealing weapons."

"So we just leave them down there for slaughter?" Susan asked.

"Who knows what they are going to do with those cannibals. Like you said before, leverage."

"They're not cannibals. News reports are saying that they're reanimated corpses. All they do is feed…on us living human beings," Susan responded. "With or without you, sir, I am going down to block B to see what's going on."

The warden sighed and responded, "I'm sorry, Officer Wells, but my choice is final, and besides my chopper is already on its way to pick me up." Unitas came from a family of wealth. His father had been the warden a generation earlier, and the title had been passed down to his son, who obviously was not well suited for the position—nepotism at its worst.

"So that's it?" Wells asked.

"I'm afraid so, Susan. I have family, a real family outside of these walls, and I need to be with them. There is nothing more I can do here."

"You know, Warden…I used to look up to you, but seeing your true colors come out now, I can honestly say that I have lost all respect for you," Susan said with her eyes welling up with tears. She continued, "I'm going down there. Those are my friends that they have. You can just stay cozy in your office—it's what you're best at." She left the office and slammed the door behind her. She began her trek down to cellblock B, and at that point, she was expecting to walk in on a massacre. Susan Wells was going to find out.

Transformation

Nausea set in intensely. My breathing had become labored as the chilled sweat soaked all my clothing. Internally, my body felt like a furnace. The jolts and violent tremors in my neck were sporadic. My eyelids fluttered uncontrollably, and my limbs and fingers twitched with no letup—it felt like an oncoming seizure. All the muscles in my body began to tighten up and cramp, making it difficult to extend my hands from the onset of atrophy. I was certain I had been in and out of consciousness for at least an hour, only being awakened from the screams and hollering of the surrounding inmates.

As I sat up against the back wall, I could see four men standing, not too far outside the cell door. One of the men was armed. The shackled guard that had been seated in front of the cell earlier was nowhere in sight. He must have been moved while I was out. Whether he was alive or dead, I didn't know. Standing in his place was a prisoner held at gunpoint.

"We don't want you interacting with any of the other men. You can stay in this cell until you've cooled off. This guy in here seems fine...well, alive anyway," the man with the gun said to the other prisoner. I had not caught either of their names, but they had caught my attention...it was my cell that he was talking about.

"So you don't even have the balls to kill me. You're gonna keep me around, hoping that I'll be cured overnight? That's why you won't make it through this thing alive, Vince...you don't know how to be selfish...you don't know how to survive."

"Well, I've made it in here this long with pieces of shit like you. Think I'll be fine. Bernie, open the cell, please." Carlos must have been the one lashing out against the officers earlier—I recognized his voice.

The door opened, and Vince, the man with the gun, guided Carlos forward a couple of feet. I remained silent and backed myself into the corner of the cell where most light was absent. I must have come off like a timid, stray dog. Carlos pulled away from the loose grip Vince had on his right arm and stepped into the room voluntarily. With the prisoner entering the cell, my anxiety increased, and I could feel my heart pounding rapidly. The blood coursing through my body rushed to my head and caused another sudden wave of nausea. Before I could attempt to calm myself, I had already begun to nod in and out…and then the familiar dark.

* * * * *

"Hey, man, are you okay?"

I heard the voice say as I was awakened from repeated nudges to my inner shoulder. My eyes slowly opened up, and I could see the man kneeling a couple of feet away, staring at me with a self-concerned expression. I recognized his face, but his name had completely gone from my mind. I tried to vocalize a response, but all that emerged were incoherent mumblings, and though I was able to vaguely think to myself, my ability to form words or sentences had seemed to vanish. As I tried to recall past occurrences, my mind immediately began to fire off blanks. The sudden loss of memory was similar to forgetting how to spell simple words while caught in a drunken stupor, and it was instant when I began to lose perspective of where I was and how I got there.

"Shit, you don't look too good, bro, you're pale as fuck," the man said, getting up from his knees as he backed away cautiously.

I could sense his fear, and the smell coming off him was interesting. My appetite was nonexistent, but an overwhelming craving for meat came over me…and I could sense a warm, fresh batch within the four walls.

I propped my right arm up on the lower bunk, just beside me, and pulled myself up to one knee, which proved to be difficult. All my joints had stiffened, and the pain running through my bones and muscles slowed me down quite a bit, but something internal kept me going.

The man in the cell with me stood with his chest against the metal bars with his hands grasped tightly to them. "Vince, get me out of here!" he yelled. "This guy doesn't look right. Just put me in another cell…Vince?" No one was responding, and no one appeared to be in close proximity.

I got up to my feet and began to move forward. As I took each step, I noticed that my chest wasn't expanding from respiration…I was no longer breathing. But even so, this newfound animalistic instinct kept me from stopping. My feet dragged themselves across the floor, yet he didn't notice me until I stumbled from the weakness in my ankles. He turned his head as I fell forward, but I caught myself on the back of his prison jumpsuit. He struggled to turn around, but my body weight had him pinned against the bars.

I was partially hunched over, and before I even thought to look up, the hunger for warm, fresh meat lured my snapping jaws to his fleshy, lower backside. The force from the bite was strong enough to tear through the fabric and break the skin, drawing first blood. I sank my teeth farther down into the torn flesh and pushed away from his body with my hands, planted on his calves, forcing him down to his knees. He yelled something, but I did not hear what—profanities of some kind. The bloodlust had my focus drawn to his open wound and the meat that I was chewing on. My first taste of human flesh calmed my craving just enough as if I were a dope fiend shooting up heroin after a severe episode of withdrawal.

It was all I could think of. The horrendous view of the macabre seemed to fuel my animalistic instincts, and all that I wanted to do from that point on was eat. My remaining thoughts began to leave my mind as I continued to feed. I had truly become lost in the gruesome acts I had just committed as if nothing else seemed to matter. I had become a flesh-eating monster…for good. A complete transformation into an undead mindset—a reanimated corpse—and I knew that there was no hope of a reversal. The man I had fed on was most certainly gone based on the copious amounts of blood he had lost through his initial wound. I reached into the open cavity and continued to extract organs to gorge upon, including the liver and one of his kidneys. My humanity had been officially lost, and my days as a living human being would cease to exist. The horrific events would continue to snowball until the time presented itself for me to get taken out by someone else. God willing, it wouldn't be long.

Held Up

Susan Wells passed through the connecting corridor which led her from cellblock A to cellblock B. Streaks of dry blood ran along the walls, and she noticed from some of the areas that they had been left behind by a set of hands. She approached the entrance to the sally port and saw that the smears of blood had stopped at the end corner of the corridor and then reappeared on the face of the grimy-looking metal door, with a smudged handprint that made its track to the left and ended near the edge of the entry. Susan peered through the small window that allowed a view into the port but saw nothing and no one inside. She pushed a small button to her left with a rectangular metal faceplate. The button was used to buzzed in to gain access to the block.

"Who the hell is that?" said Gringo. Vince hovered in front of one of the several monitors sitting above the control panel; they were back in the control room. The monitor showed the outside of the cellblock entrance, and the female officer was in sight. Bernie and Gringo stood close by while Officer Vicks and Officer Fredericks sat toward the back of the room, bound to their chairs. The duct tape had been removed from their mouths by the three inmates.

"It's another guard, looks like a woman," Vince said.

"Her name is Susan Wells, a CO from block A," Fredericks explained.

"What is she doing here?" Gringo said alarmingly.

Bernie sighed and sat down in one of the swivel chairs near the panel. He rested his eyes and kept to himself for the time being.

"I'm guessing that since we haven't had any contact with the other officers in over an hour, she probably came down here to check on the status of this block. I suggest you let her in," Fredericks said.

"Nah, nah, don't let her in, Vince, she'll just lock us back up," Gringo said in an anxious tone. He began pacing in small steps.

Vince continued to look at the monitor and noticed that the guard pull a set of keys off her belt loop. "I don't think we have a choice. She has a key to get into the sally port, and I'm almost certain that that same key will get her into the block. It won't take her long, but she better watch herself with all of the other prisoners out there…they'll be on her like a pack of hyenas."

"That won't be a problem," Fredericks said. "She's dealt with worse situations than this before and knows how to take care of herself. She's a tough cookie."

"Son of a bitch," Susan said under her breath. She was unlocking the sally port entrance manually. After removing the key from the lock, she pulled the weighty metal slab open and noticed that the blood went from the outside edge of the door to the inside edge on the opposite side. Susan looked ahead as she walked through the doorway and saw more of the same—two blood-smeared handprints on the surface of the entrance to the cellblock. Her first inclination was to reach for her pistol. She placed her right hand on the gun handle and unbuttoned the strap of the holster by flicking her thumb upward.

She then grabbed her radio with her free hand and said, "This is Officer Wells to Emergency Response Team. We have a possible breach in cellblock A. I repeat, a possible breach in cellblock A. I need you to standby and prepare to engage."

Susan brought the radio up to her ear, anticipating a response. After about five seconds of silence, she realized that no one was on the other end—at least no one willing to act. She hooked the small radio back onto the shoulder loop, which was attached to her uniform. Before unlocking the second door herself, she held her position for a few moment to see if there were any other officers inside. Someone would have been sure to see her on the monitor screen by that point.

"She's inside the port, but she's just standing there," said Vince, keeping his eyes locked on the screen.

"Vince, if she makes it past the other inmates and wants inside, we can't let her," Gringo said. Vince didn't say anything; he just lightly shook his head in disagreement. "Did you hear me, Vince? We've already got two other—"

"Will you shut up, man," Bernie said, cutting Gringo off. "If she makes it to the outside of that door," Bernie pointed to the control room entrance, "then we're gonna let her in…no one else needs to die."

"If she's smart, she won't come in at all. Hopefully, after seeing everyone out of their cells, she'll turn the other way and leave," Vince said, responding to Bernie.

Susan approached the entrance door and looked through a second glass window into the cellblock. She could see that many of the cells were open from the front of the corridor, leading all the way down to the opposite side where a group of prisoners surrounded the outside of the control room. It quickly became apparent to her that she was going to have to let herself in, and that moment seemed like the perfect time to do so with the prisoners' attention being drawn to whatever it was inside that room. Susan gently slid the key into the lock and turned it, disengaging the lock as quietly as she could. She pushed the door outward, away from her, and slid in through the opening, being careful not to let the metal slab slam shut behind her. None of the inmates inside the block seemed to have noticed—no one had heard her come in.

The gun was being held at her waist side. She glanced at each cell on both sides of her as she slowly walked down the block. The prisoners that remained in their cells seemed docile enough. They just stared at her with dumbfounded looks on their faces as she continued moving down the corridor. Susan raised her left index finger up to her mouth to signal the men to remain quiet. She followed this motion with a slight raise of her gun, just high enough for the inmates to see that she was armed. This seemed to have worked because they didn't make a sound.

As Susan made her way farther down the block, she glanced over to her right and immediately noticed three darkened cells that sat side by side to each other on the opposite end of the corridor, closer to the control room. The first of the rooms held a body, dragging itself across the floor which was covered in blood. The man maneuvered himself around a limp object where the blood seemed to be coming from. Susan's eyes adjusted to the darkness as she peered in closer inside the cell, attempting to identify what exactly it was that she was looking at. The forms of two human figures began to gradually reveal themselves. *What the hell is that man eating?* Susan thought to herself, baffled and disgusted. She was unable to discern whose bodies they were, which had her concerned, knowing that the prisoners had been out of their cells for quite some time, and she still had not come across any of the other officers.

The second room wasn't much different than the first. Blood covered the floors, from what Susan could only assume came from another cannibalistic-like feeding session. She proceeded toward the control room and the group of inmates who were grouped outside the door and window.

"Back away from the door and move to the side, all of you!" Susan shouted, with her Beretta pointed at the men.

The prisoners raging at the entrance of the control room abruptly stopped and slowly turned around, only to be pleasantly surprised at the sight of a woman in their presence. Several of the men looked at her with perverted grins on their faces, almost being driven to the point of salivating.

"Hey, *hermosa*, you know how to use that piece? 'Cause I know how to use mine, baby," one of the prisoners said while grabbing his groin. He then moved his crotch up and down with his right hand.

Susan ignored the crude gesture, took two steps forward, and said, "I'm not your baby, goddammit. Now put your hands where I can see them and back the fuck away!"

The group of men parted into two smaller groups, simultaneously gravitating to the opposite sides of the entrance door, some with their hands at their waist side with palms facing outward while others remained as they were, unfazed by the female guard. Susan moved ahead in between the two small groups, slowly shifting her body while the barrel of her pistol swayed to the right in a half circle, moving from inmate to inmate. Her heart rate had increased significantly, and the anxiety began to weigh heavily on her entire body as she was being surrounded by sixteen convicted lifers. She took three final steps back before reaching the control room entrance. The sudden halt from the cold steel door startled Susan as her spine pressed against the solid outer surface, causing her to jump in place, but she was still able to keep her defenses up.

Three pounding knocks emerged from outside the control room. "She's outside the door, you gotta let her in," said Vicks.

"Don't do it. She's just gonna throw us back out there," Gringo said as he looked through the window at the gang of rabid men. He turned back to Vince. "And our chances of staying alive aren't looking too great right now."

"Maybe if we let her in, she'll help us," Vince said.

"You gotta be kidding, right? We have two officers tied up in here, and you think that she's going to have mercy on us? We'll be lucky if being thrown in segregation is the worst of it," Gringo replied.

Three more pounding knocks were heard, followed by a woman's voice shouting, "Hurry the fuck up and let me in!" Susan had been reduced to pleading, realizing she couldn't hold off the prisoners much longer.

"Open the door already. They're going to tear her apart out there!" Vicks shouted.

"Bullshit. He told us she could take care of herself," said Gringo, looking over at Fredericks.

Vince stood motionless near the control panel with his right hand planted on his forehead. He tuned the others out, trying to figure out what to do.

Vicks sighed and said, "I heard what he fucking told you, but she's outnumbered, and they have her barricaded in...she won't make it out of the block alive."

Bernie peered out at the inmates as they closed in on Susan and then glanced around the room at the four others, only to see that nothing productive was being done. When no one was paying attention, he slid his hand over to the switch that unlocked the control room door, allowing Susan to push her way in. Her back was facing the five men as she entered the confined space quickly. Once the door had shut, Susan came to a stop. She took a brief moment to recuperate and began breathing heavily. Vince, Bernie, Gringo, and the two restrained officers watched her in silence, waiting in anticipation for her to share any available information she may have had of the events taking place elsewhere in the prison. Susan remained quiet, not even acknowledging their presence. Her head hung low with her eyes closed. The gun that she was holding was still armed. Her finger did not once leave the trigger, just as a precaution.

Vince gazed at Susan, not knowing what to say. Although he was relieved that she had made it inside and unscathed, he still felt a sense of guilt for prolonging the process of allowing her to enter. It was at that moment when Vince realized how fortunate he was to have someone like Bernie in his corner, being able to make the decision to spare her life when no one else wanted to act.

Gringo turned to face the back wall, away from the others, with his hands propped on his waist, pissed off that his suggestion to keep the female officer out had gone unheeded. Though he had broken free from Carlos's grasp, he still felt as if he was being viewed by his two fellow inmates as a weak individual when in fact, for the most part, his intentions seemed incomprehensible to his peers, which had been the main reason his suggestions were going unacknowledged.

Once Susan had gathered her breath, she finally scanned her surroundings. It became obvious to her that Vince, Bernie, and Gringo were taking refuge in the control room for protection from the other prisoners and that they proposed no immediate threat to her wellbeing—they were just scared—and so began her questioning.

"Before I even get into what took you pricks so long to open the door, first I need to know why there are two COs tied up. And how the fuck did you three and the other inmates manage to get out of your cells?" Susan said as she scanned the entirety of the room. Simultaneous to that, she wiped the sweat from her forehead with the same hand that she held her pistol with. She smirked and let out a single condescending laugh. "Obviously, neither of you three is in control of the situation," Susan said. She glared at Vince, Bernie, and Gringo and continued. "You see those men out there?" She pointed out the window and into the cellblock. "They're in control now. They have us boxed in here like dogs in a kennel, and they're showing no signs of letup."

"It was Vince. The son of a bitch knocked me out and cuffed me to the guardrail on the second tier," said Fredericks.

Susan glanced over at Vince and said, "Is that true? Did you attack Fredericks?"

"I had no choice. He came into my cell, accused me of something that I had nothing to do with, and then became physically abusive," Vince replied.

Fredericks shook his head in disagreement and said, "I barely nudged him, besides the little shit was being noncompliant during my questioning."

"That's bullshit. You consider throwing me off of my bunk barely nudging? You've treated all of the inmates like trash, so yeah, I did what I had to because obviously nothing was being done to stop the mistreatment of the prisoners here."

Susan shifted her glare over to Fredericks and Vicks in complete shock from what she was hearing.

"So what? Are you going to get us out of these restraints?" Fredericks asked, expecting her not to believe in the words of a man who had been convicted of murder.

She hesitated for a brief moment, and then made her way over to the two COs strapped into the wooden chairs. She stopped in front of Vicks, kneeled down on one knee, and began unraveling the duct tape, freeing his ankles. Next were his wrists. He got up to his feet slowly and stumbled a bit. Susan grabbed Vicks by the shoulders, stood him up straight, and held him in place until he got some of his strength back. Being seated for such an extensive amount of time had weakened his legs.

"Thank you," Vicks said as he stretched out his back. He took in a deep breath, let out a sigh of relief, and then began walking around the room to get the circulation in his legs going.

"Were you present when the abuse took place against Morris?" Susan asked Vicks as he was walking away.

"No, I wasn't. I had been ordered by Fredericks to go outside and collect the bodies of Officer Sanchez and Officer Ramon," he responded while still in motion as he paced around.

Susan sighed and said, "And when were you taken hostage by these guys?" She motioned her head over to Vince and Bernie. Gringo was sitting on the floor against the wall in the back of the room with his arms crossed on top of his knees.

Vicks stopped in place, looked over his shoulder, and said, "Actually, they were the ones who saved me." He resumed walking. "I would for sure be dead right now if it wasn't for them bringing me in here. Same goes for Fredericks."

"And the fact that they had you strapped to a chair makes no difference?" asked Susan.

"These guys weren't responsible for that," Vicks responded.

Vince and Bernie refrained from speaking and just stood back and observed, with the sole purpose of cooperating with the female officer, trying not to test the waters any further than they had already been tested.

"Well, who was it that took you guys hostage?" Susan asked.

Before Vicks could answer, Gringo spoke up. "It was Carlos. That piece of shit held the guards at gunpoint and cuffed their hands behind their backs. When one of them tried retaliating, he shot and killed him."

"And where's Carlos now?" said Susan.

"Don't worry about it, he's not a problem," Gringo replied in a monotone voice.

Susan paused, turned around, and looked out the window to check the status of the prisoners' behavior. Seeing that they had begun easing up as they slowly disbanded away from the door, she turned back to Gringo. "I need to know if he's still in the block. If he's just going around killing my guys, then I can't be caught up in here for very long."

Gringo did not respond, planting his face down onto his forearms still rested on his knees. He had been locked up long enough to know that he had already said too much. "Stitches end up in ditches" was the phrase that came to Gringo's mind—a phrase that the majority of prisoners lived by in pretty much every penitentiary in the United States. And more so he had a newfound respect for Vince and felt the obligation to not say another word.

"What's your name?" Susan said to Gringo, putting the good cop technique into play. He remained silent. "Goddammit, I don't have time for your prison politics bullshit! I have to get back to my block and let the others know about this." She bolted for the door.

Vince looked over to his left at Bernie. He looked Vince in the eyes and gave him a head nod, not having to say a word. And as if Vince could read Bernie's mind, he went after Susan, grabbed her arm, and said, "Wait, I can expl—"

She jerked away from his grasp, turned, and quickly raised her pistol, aiming it at Vince's face in high alert.

"Whoa, it's fine, it's fine," said Vince with his hands raised to his shoulders. "You don't have to worry about Carlos. We have him locked up in one of the cells. Just don't go back out there, they'll kill you."

Susan looked at Vince, unamused. She lowered her gun and loosened her stance. "What the fuck do you care if I get killed or not? I'm the enemy in here," Susan said as she walked over to an empty chair with her shoulders slumped. She took a seat.

"Look, I'm sorry about your friends, but you just can't assume that everyone in here is against you. I couldn't stop Carlos from killing the other guards, but we were able to get Vicks out of there. That should tell you something about what our intentions are," Vince replied.

"That's all good and fine, and I thank you for what you did, but why let everyone out of their cells?" Susan said.

"I wanted to show these guys that we all stand on equal ground. If I have a chance to make it out of here, why not them too?"

"Because most of these guys actually belong here," said Vicks. "We understand that you don't mean any harm, but you just can't go around giving everyone the benefit of the doubt and assume that this place has changed these guys for the better."

"But with everything that's been going on out there, we all deserve to know if our people on the outside are okay. Seems like the world is going to hell out there," Vince said.

Vicks sat back down, shook his head in slight agreement, and stared at the ground as he bit his bottom lip, caught in a moment of thought. He looked back over at Susan. "Any news from your end?"

Susan wore an unresponsive expression on her face, dumbfounded by the question. "Well, we've lost the warden, but other than that, I know just as much as you guys, probably less."

"Dead?" said Vicks.

"No, he's alive, just sitting this one out. Saw everything that was going on around him and just couldn't take it," Susan responded. She got up from the chair and glanced around at everybody in the room. "Seems like cellblock A has been the life of the party, so why don't you fill me in on what's going on."

"They're dead," said Bernie.

Susan, caught off guard, turned her attention toward the soft-spoken man. "I know they are. Carlos killed them. Are you feeling all right?"

"No, those things out there that they were feeding...they're dead."

She gave Vince a puzzled look. "He's right. I heard it on the radio. Don't you guys keep up with the broadcasts? Locally at least?" Vince said.

"No, things in here generally keep us pretty busy. Today has been no exception," Susan replied.

"Apparently the recently deceased are coming back to life. And this is happening all over the world. Sounds like some sort of global miracle is happening, right?" Vince raised his eyebrows, showing false intrigue. "Not so much. They attack and kill anything that's breathing."

"More like something out of revelations," said Gringo.

Vince peered over his shoulder in response to his fellow inmate. He turned back to Susan and shook his head, confirming the observation.

"I don't buy it. You're talking about something supernatural at work here, an act of God," said Susan.

"After seeing a man walk around who had been pronounced dead from a heart attack only days before, you'd be feeling differently right now," Bernie replied.

"And you can't mistake the smell of a dead body," Vince added.

Vicks leaned forward in his chair and said, "They're right, Susan. I was outside when they began collecting outside of the fence, that smell was almost unbearable. Whatever those things are, they're not living."

"Now that they're in, we have to get back to cellblock B and get this area contained. We can only do that from outside of this block with the resources that we can't get to from in here," said Susan.

"How did you know they got in?" asked Vicks.

"Unitas saw everything from his window."

"And he didn't—" Vicks cut himself off, bringing a clenched fist to his mouth in frustration.

"I told you he's gone," Susan replied.

"I hate to interrupt, but when one of you get the chance, would you mind getting me out of this fucking chair?" Fredericks said.

Susan turned to the restrained CO and with a smirk on her face, said, "Sounds like you've been busy lately. I think you've earned a break."

He went limp in his chair, looked up at the ceiling, and muttered, "You've gotta be fucking kidding me."

"There are at least a dozen prisoners out there that want us dead, Susan, all of us. We're gonna have to take these guys with us if we want to get through to the other end of the block," Vicks suggested.

"Right. I am not going to willingly open fire unless the circumstances absolutely call for it. I made it through the first time in one piece, the six of us should do fine," Susan replied.

Bernie saw the wariness in her eyes and said, "Let them out."

Vince paused and looked at him, puzzled. Gringo had a similar expression but only because he had not clearly heard what Bernie had said from the back of the room. Vicks and Susan gave each other a quick glance and shrugged their shoulders with an unspoken understanding that they were both willing to listen to whatever suggestions were going to be given out by the inmates. Fredericks had checked out, throwing himself a pity party from the comfort of his chair.

Vince peered out the window and said, "They had their chance to escape, but they chose to stay here. What makes you think they are going to leave now?"

"I'm not talking about the other men," Bernie said.

"You're holding 'em in the cells, aren't you? I saw the bodies when I came into the block," said Susan.

"That wasn't our call," Vince said.

"So they really do eat people," Susan said.

Vince lowered his head with his eyes closed and said, "Carlos was using them as a weapon, feeding the guards to them."

"And more than likely they'll attack once outa the cells," Bernie said in response to Susan.

Gringo got up to his feet and approached the others. "That won't be enough. There are only four of them and over a dozen inmates."

"That's all we'll need. Just enough to keep them occupied so we can pass right through," Bernie replied.

"What about the noise?" Vince said. "As soon as those cell doors open, those guys will hear what's going on. Besides they are all pretty well spread out. Giving them a perfect view of those cells, it would be a waste of time."

"We'll open the control room door and draw them back over here," Susan said. She walked over to the control panel, rested her hands on the board, and looked out the window. "Once the prisoners are gathered outside the door, we'll open the cells holding those things. That should free up enough space for us to get through to the other side…if they do what we want them to do."

Vince looked around the room, nodding his head, and said, "That's as good of a plan as any, I guess."

"That's the only plan. If you have anything else in mind, let us know," Susan said.

"Hell, as long as it's not us going back in those cages," Gringo said.

"We will discuss that later," Susan said with a stern look. She turned back to the others. "Which cells are they being held in?"

"Over there, nineteen and twenty," Vince replied, pointing out at the two darkened cells.

Susan peered out through the window to where Vince was pointing and then began to pace at a slow but steady speed. "Okay, once the door is open, we have to get their attention to let them know we're coming out. They should come right at us and, hopefully, won't see the attack coming."

"We're going to have to move quickly once out of the room," Vicks added.

"Yeah, no shit," Fredericks said with a snicker. "You going to uncuff me or just leave me here to die?"

Susan walked over to where he was sitting and said, "You know, I was really considering the latter after the shit you pulled, but we are going to need every able-bodied person we can get." She unlatched the set of keys from her belt loop, went behind him, and proceeded to loosen and remove the restraints. "I'm only going to say this once. You mistreat anyone else in this group or try anything else while we're trying to make it out of here…you're done. I will make sure that we never cross paths again after we leave you behind, understand? I have no doubt in my mind that you will wind up dead."

Fredericks paused for a moment, turned his head, glared at Susan, and said, "Yeah, sure, understood." And his glare shifted into an unnerving grin.

Escape

Susan stood at the control room entrance with a tight grip on the door handle. She turned to Vicks and said, "Once I crack the door open, I'll let you know when those guys are on the move. When they get close enough, I'll signal you to open the two cells."

Vicks hovered over the control panel. Vince, Bernie, and Gringo were standing just behind Susan, eager to get moving before any more doubts over their operation could form. Fredericks stood farther back in the room just behind the others with his arms crossed.

"Unlock the entrance door to the cellblock," Susan said in a monotone voice. As she peered out the small rectangular window to the door, her breath began to fog up the pane of glass, recalling the instance of terror she had experienced from her last tour through the block. *Just calm down and stay focused,* Susan thought to herself.

The latch to the door clicked. Once unlocked, the noise echoed through the entire corridor down to the opposite end where the control room was located. Every inmate heard the distinct sound and immediately knew what it was. Already on edge, their attention turned to the entrance door, anticipating the arrival of more prison staff, but none of them moved. These men were not ignorant to their surroundings and took every noise or visual as a potential distraction to be taken out.

"We have to move soon," said Susan. "Those doors only stay unlocked for a few minutes, if that." She looked back at the others. "You boys ready?" Vince, Bernie, and Gringo glanced at each other and turned to Susan with pale, hollow expressions on their faces. After a brief moment, Vince gave her the head nod. Gringo's stomach turned, and he took a few steps back in hesitation, but Bernie pulled him back into the group. At that point, backing out was no longer an option. The prisoners had been triggered, and the floodgates were about to be opened.

"Vicks, on three, unlock my door. Don't hesitate," ordered Susan while she kept her focus on the outside. A handful of the men still had their eye on the control room, keeping close watch on the group inside.

"I'm on it," Vicks replied with an apparent urgency in his voice. Beads of sweat had formed on his forehead and began inching closer to his brow.

A similar sensation was shared throughout the room as the critical moment drew closer. The realization of how severe the situation was bubbled up to the surface of their consciousness. Of course, they had known this the entire time but chose to put it out of their minds up until the final moments had arrived and the plan began to come to fruition. Fredericks resorted to sitting back down. In his mind he had four human shields for protection. Out of spite, he began rocking his chair back and forth and waited patiently to watch it all fall apart.

Susan took a deep breath and began to countdown. "One… two…" Bernie bowed his head and said a prayer, making the sign of the cross, from head to chest then shoulder to shoulder. "Three. Unlock my door, Officer Vicks."

Vicks flipped the switch labeled UNLOCK, which branched off a blueprint image of the control room. Susan felt the vibration in the door handle from the clicking of the latch. With delicate force, she cracked the heavy metal slab open, expecting to see the prisoners on the other side react…they didn't take notice. "They're not budging," Susan said.

She continued to open the door with more force, hoping to cause the hinges to squeak. The weight from the door and the momentum from her pull did the job, putting more stress and pressure on the old rusted hinges. The noise that emerged traveled fast. The inmate closest to the control room heard the invasive squeak. His head snapped over to his right in response to what he had heard. He could see Susan through the opening, which grew larger in the door. Many of the other inmates had stopped paying attention after congregating into different groups and were, at that point, getting high and shooting the shit. Though there were still several others watching the entrance to the cellblock like guard dogs. No one was going to get in, no one was going to get out—not in their house.

"Open those cells now!" Susan shouted. "They'll be coming." Distracted, Vicks was looking out the window to see where the inmates were positioned, trying to visualize a potential pathway through the corridor and its inhabitants. Susan moved her head back and forth from the opening in the door to her fellow officer who was standing to her left. "Vicks, open the fucking cells, now!"

The prisoner began to approach at fast pace, followed by six others who had taken notice of the situation after hearing Susan bark her orders. All the closed cells on the first floor opened at once, but the men kept coming, caught in an adrenalized state. The noise from the opening gates seemed to go unheeded. Susan pulled the door closed in one swift motion. The first inmate slammed into the outer face of the metal slab just as it was being shut. He began to pound on the surface with the base of his palms.

"COME ON, COME ON! WE JUST WANNA PLAY!" he shouted through the small window. The glass began to collect condensation from the man's heavy breath.

Susan inched her head back, turned to the side, and closed her eyes. The other six prisoners were close behind, collecting outside the door and the main window, which looked into the control room. Farther back, behind them, two bodies of the reanimated wandered from out of the cells, fresh from their awakening. Their initiators followed, with one leaving a smeared trail of blood in its wake as it crawled along the concrete floor.

"You're gonna have to come out of there at some point," said the inmate at the door. "You can't just stay in that room while the rest of the world goes to shit around us. It don't matter how long you keep your heads in the sand…we ain't goin' nowhere."

They looked into each other eyes as the tension between the two permeated outward. Susan shifted her line of sight to below their waistlines, past their legs, and then smirked. He followed her cue and looked back at the ground. "Watch out behind you!" the inmate shouted.

Creeping along the floor, the emaciated body latched onto the upper ankle of the prisoner in the back of the group. Its decaying fingers tore into the skin and muscle of his lower calf, bringing the man down to his knees. He collapsed and fell face-first as the creature pulled itself closer to the injured limb with its digits hooked into the flesh like a hawk's talons tearing through a fish. The fallen inmate tried to free himself from the grasp by kicking the soulless corpse in the face with his other foot, but the defense did not have any visible effect. The more he struggled with the attacker, the deeper the claw-like fingers sank into the fibers and tissue of his leg. Blood began to pool up.

The assailant went directly for the Achilles tendon, biting down hard with precision and ferocity. Its head began to thrash from side to side in order to free as much meat as possible. More blood was dispersed, and the connective tissue snapped as the creature pulled back from the gaping wound. One of the other inmates jerked his body in the opposite direction in an attempt to flee but was stopped short by another corpse that was quick to come up from behind. Driven by its instinct, the creature seized the man's face with both hands and with its intense strength—surprising strength—turned his head and chomped down onto his right ear. The corpse gnawed on the cartilage for a moment before the ear was completely separated from the skull.

The others stood by in shock while their "tough guy" façade dissipated, being taken aback by the vicious attack. Two of them were able to break away from the group. They ran to the opposite end of the corridor and took refuge in one of the open cells. The ringleader, who had been taunting Susan, had his back against the door, frozen with fear as the last two walking cadavers closed in. Off to his right were the two remaining prisoners from the group caught in a similar state of fear.

"Vince, help me real quick," Susan said. Vince looked at Bernie and shrugged. He approached the door and stood beside her. "Get ready to unlock this door again." Susan met eyes with Vicks, and he nodded his head.

"What are we doing?" asked Vince.

"When I open the door, this son of a bitch is gonna fall back. I want you to catch him and throw his ass back out, within reach of those two things." She looked back at Bernie and Gringo. "You two back him up in case he starts to squirm."

"My pleasure," Gringo replied.

Bernie turned to his fellow inmate and could sense his spiteful demeanor. *Man's gonna get himself killed,* he thought to himself. Shaking his head, he brushed the thought off. *It's not my place to say anything.*

"Hit the main entrance lock one more time," Susan ordered. Vicks flipped the switch. "Let's move with a purpose. Go for it, Vicks." He disengaged the control room lock and the latch clicked once again. Susan pulled the door open with force. The inmate stumbled back a few steps through the doorway. Vince went to catch him, but Gringo came up fast, pushing hard on the man's back with both of his forearms.

"Gringo, what the hell are you doing!" Vince shouted.

His momentum amped up fast, though, forcing the man forward with no chance for him to gain his bearings. The two prisoners went out into the cellblock, leaving Vince behind. Gringo didn't even bother to look at where he was going, having his eyes closed as he pushed ahead. The man on the frontline began to show some resistance. He turned himself around, enough to where he could put up a defense against Gringo. The two inmates locked arms as they plodded onward, step by step. Their pace had slowed down due to the struggle.

The blood seeping out from the man's ankle wound spread across the floor space surrounding the attack at a fast rate. The heavy loss of blood from the peroneal artery caused the prisoner to die before the corpse could even finish its feeding.

The creatures seemed to engage and respond more in the consumption of the flesh while their prey was breathing and still had a pulse. There was something about the fight being put up that would trigger their most primal animalistic instincts, but considering they were once human, the process of the attacks would target their pleasure center more so, releasing the last remnants of endorphins and mimicking the chemical reaction that occurs during sex. Once the victim was void of life, the creatures would move on to seek out their next high. The farther along they would get into the stages of decomposition, the less efficient their actions would become as they would feel no effect, chemically, from the feedings due to the complete depletion of the endorphins. The victim would be finished off, limiting their mobility and function for when they too would eventually reanimate.

The two inmates, locked in a grapple, trudged into the puddle of blood as they continued to scuffle, causing them to lose their footing. A hand grabbed onto the leg of the man in front, and for a brief moment, a wave of relief washed over him as he felt the sensation similar to that of someone being caught by a safety net after being in free fall. He looked down and could see that it was quite the contrary of a helping hand. His eyesight shifted into tunnel vision, and all that he could concentrate on were the bloodied teeth from the snapping jaws of the crawling monstrosity. The corpse tightened its grip around the cloth of the inmate's pant leg. Unstable and nauseated from his growing panic and the foul stench of the decaying flesh, the prisoner's body began to teeter back and forth. Gringo held on to the man to try to keep him upright but more so that he himself would not take a tumble. When he did inevitably collapse, Gringo released his grip and pulled his arms back, but the man's reflex was too quick. Midway to the floor, he snagged Gringo's collar with fight-or-flight strength, and they both went down.

"Son of a bitch," Bernie said under his breath as the group looked on from the control room. He bolted out through the doorway and into the block, seeming to disregard everything that was happening around him. His anticipation for Gringo's foolish behavior had prepared him enough to venture into the thick of the threat with no hesitance. His focus remained ahead to the task at hand as he pounded through the corridor.

Vince turned to Susan and said, "What do we do?" She didn't respond right away.

Bernie approached the two fallen prisoners and reached down swiftly to grab Gringo. When he had a good handle on his upper body, the inmate pinned underneath latched onto Bernie's forearm, weakening his stance and bringing him down to one knee.

"Pull me up! Pull me u—" The prisoner bellowed but was cut off when the corpse locked its mandible over his mouth, being drawn to the heat and noise emitting from the opening. Its teeth sank into the skin near the base of his cheeks and jowls. When blood began to surface, the creature fastened its jaws and started to pull back slowly, tearing the flesh of the man's upper lip away from the gums and teeth. In one swift jerk, he pulled Bernie closer in as a reaction to the excruciating pain he was experiencing just before going into shock.

"Fuck this, I'm going out there," Vince said as he rushed through the doorway past Susan.

Susan looked at Vicks with an anxious look on her face and said, "And now we go." She moved out from behind the door and entered the cellblock at a fast pace to where she was trailing just behind Vince. She raised her gun and began panning from side to side as she passed the first two cells on both sides of her.

"Let's go," Vicks said to Fredericks. Fredericks stood up from his chair and sauntered over. Vicks charged toward him and said, "Come on, man, I mean it." He grabbed his upper arm and pulled him along out of the control room.

The inmate's grip on Bernie's forearm loosened as his blood pressure dropped and his body went limp. Bernie watched in horror being so close to the gore as more of the man's facial tissue was removed from the area surrounding the initial wound, and then he jumped, being startled, when he felt something touch his shoulder. He turned his head and was relieved to see that it was Vince.

"We gotta go," he said as he extended his right hand out to Bernie.

"Right," Bernie replied. He placed both hands on his raised knee and pushed himself up to his feet, in no need of Vince's assistance. Susan passed by them with her pistol still raised, putting herself at the head of the group just as she had originally planned in her head. Gringo was sitting on the floor, upright and out of breath. Vince grabbed him by his sleeve and yanked him up. Gringo stabilized himself after the sudden motion and stood firm. Vince looked at him with disappointment and just shook his head.

Gringo shamefully grinned, shrugged, and said, "Heh, sorry."

Bernie turned to the rueful inmate, pointed his index finger at his face, and said, "I'll deal with you later…if we make it out of this."

Vince peered around the block and noticed that two more of the undead were in pursuit, coming in from the sides, just ahead of them, after becoming aware of their gathering. His eyes wandered back to the control room.

Fredericks came out through the doorway with Vicks right behind him. His grip remained on the narrowly compliant COs arm, but Vince could not tell whether or not he was holding a gun to his back with his other hand—a precaution he felt may have been necessary. He glanced over to the right of the two guards at the cell where he threw Carlos into, but Carlos was nowhere in sight, only a man he did not recognize could be seen, clinging to the metal bars and covered in blood. Vince was overcome with sorrow as he realized what had more than likely taken place partially by his hands. *You had no choice,* he thought but quickly brought himself out of his own head. "Come on, we gotta keep moving," he said to Bernie and Gringo, and they proceeded forward, dodging the two corpses by speeding up their pace.

All the potential human threats in the cellblock had been neutralized, and the majority of the other prisoners were stowed away in their cells, taking refuge from the danger running rampant throughout the corridor.

Susan cleared the stretch, approached the main entrance/exit, and stopped to look back. Bernie and Gringo were not far behind. Vince followed, repeatedly glancing over his shoulder until he had reached the others. Susan looked at him and saw that he was wearing a distressed look on his face.

"What is it? What's wrong?" she asked.

"Nothing…it's just…you didn't see…" Vince said as he began to turn his head. He stopped himself with a flinch and looked back at Susan, appearing confused. "It's nothing. Let's just get the hell out of here."

Vicks and Fredericks brought up the rear, and the group was back together as a unit. Susan looked over everyone just to make sure they were all accounted for. She turned around, pulled the door open, and proceeded to motion them into the sally port with her head. One by one they entered with Bernie and Gringo at the lead. Concerned, Susan kept her eyes locked on Vince as he walked past her, but he kept his head low. Vicks and Fredericks were the last to go in, and with one last glance around cellblock B, Susan shut the door behind her, and they were gone.

Awaiting Departure

It was just after dark. Warden Unitas sat at his desk with the two lamps in his office shut off. Light from the facility posts outside came in through the window, which overlooked the rec yard, allowing for enough visibility in the room to keep the warden at ease. The captain of the prison, Richard Groves, stood by, off to the side, near the entrance door. As second-in-command, he chose to uphold his duty and remain on the premises when things started to fall apart. Once the order to stand down was given by the warden, the majority of the higher-ranking officers abandoned their posts after losing faith in their leader. At that point, the captain's status of power over the men was relinquished, and the only thing that was left for him to do was to wait.

"We should get to the helipad, sir," the captain said. The warden didn't respond. He just sat in silence with his head in his hands. "Sam, did you hear what I said?"

Unitas suddenly looked up. "Do you think I made the right choice, Richard?" he asked as if the Captain's words had been disregarded.

Groves let out an irritable sigh and said, "By retreating?" The warden nodded. "Maybe not the right choice but the logical one, self-preservation, right?"

Unitas looked back at the captain, unamused with the passive-aggressive tone that had accompanied his response, and then continued speaking. "I never wanted this title, but it was an easy out. I didn't care about pleasing my father or accomplishing something for myself. I didn't have to."

Groves lightly shook his head and then tuned to look out through the window. The outdoor perimeter lights illuminated the prison grounds and the surrounding areas around the facility, revealing the undead bodies roaming near the fences—many still latched onto the chain link. They showed no sign of moving on from the property. The fevered activity with the truck being brought onto the rec yard seemed to have lure more of them in, and after becoming aware of the presence of life on the inside, they continued in their state of dwelling on the outside.

"It was just a way to make money at first, but after a while, all I wanted to do was connect with the people here, staff and inmates alike, get along with them, ya know?" Unitas said.

"Yeah, I know," Groves replied, knowing all too well of the warden's inconsistent behavior: showing compassion toward the prisoners when face-to-face with them but then, immediately after, ordering that they be scolded and disciplined as a behavioral treatment. A strategy that he used to display his position of authority but one that stemmed from his need to gain the approval and acceptance of his officers.

Ultimately Unitas's need to please both sides turned out to be an ineffective approach to running the facility, and it did not take long before the prisoners detected the warden's two-faced nature, driving them to become unresponsive to his ingenuine presence. The insubordination of those inmates led to the removal of all inmate visitation privileges after Captain Groves had convinced the warden that the best way to gain back control over his prisoners was by severing communication between them and their loved ones on the outside. Desperate for some direction, Unitas agreed, and the punishment was implemented two weeks prior to their current situation. Two weeks which consisted of outcries and protests from the families of the men being held in lockup.

"I just wanted to do right by the people here, but I'm starting to think that cutting these men off from the outside world was not the best solution," said Unitas.

"You did, but things started going to shit before we could get results," Groves replied. "All we can do now is flee, seeing that we don't have the manpower to secure this prison. No point in going down with the ship when there has never been any honor, only second-guessed decision-making."

With no response, the warden resorted back to his silence and just gazed ahead as the sense of failure began to rise up and wash over him—the failure that had been with him since his first day on the job.

Out of the quiet emerged the sound of whirling helicopter blades from outside, off in the distance. Captain Groves approached the window, looked out into the sky, and scanned the horizon. Once the helicopter was visible, he said, "That's your escort, sir, we've gotta go."

Unitas peered up at the ceiling and could hear the sound of the blades moving over the top of the building toward the back of the facility where the helipad was located. He raised himself out of his chair and walked over to the office door. "What about your briefcase, sir?" asked the captain.

The warden looked back at his desk where the case containing unfinished summary reports and the documents for new prisoner intakes was lying front side down on the oak surface. He turned away and said, "I won't be needing it."

Groves approached his boss and said, "I'll go out first to make sure it's all clear out there. Just stay behind me." Unitas nodded his head in agreement. The captain pulled the door open, put his head out into the hallway to check both sides of the corridor, and then gave the thumbs-up with his left hand, signaling the warden that it was clear. Groves glanced back at Unitas and said, "Let's go." He stepped out of the office and proceeded onward with the warden following close behind.

As the helicopter was coming in for its landing, the noise from the motor and the blades in motion traveled through the woods surrounding the penitentiary, drawing more attention from the flesh-eating creatures, many of which had been roaming the forested area prior to the events that were taking place. Simultaneously, they shifted their direction from the aimless wandering they had been lost in, to a straight route leading to the prison. One by one, the lumbering bodies emerged from the woodland as they plodded ahead and moved into the grass field. From a few miles out, more of the undead began to follow.

Their Numbers Grow

"Don't ever put me in that position again," said Bernie. He had Gringo pushed back against the wall at the halfway point of the corridor between cellblock A and cellblock B. "You almost got me killed. I oughta put you on the floor."

"I know, I got carried away, man. I told you I was sorry," Gringo replied.

"That apology don't mean shit when all you can do is shrug the whole thing off. Pulling a dumb stunt like that, trying to prove something, isn't gonna make you any more of a man in this place. Deep down you're still just that scared little white boy that walked through those gates the day you arrived."

"Fuck you, Bernie!" Gringo said, stepping up to the older man with a formerly suppressed ferocity fueling his stride.

Vince quickly intervened and placed himself in between his two fellow inmates. "If you guys keep this up, we'll end up dead anyways. Now cut the bull—"

"Quiet!" Susan shouted, interrupting Vince. "Do you hear that?" The question rendered the group silent.

Susan walked over to one of the 30" × 56" corridor windows which looked out onto the backside of the penitentiary. Curious, the others followed her lead with Gringo and Fredericks approaching the window on her left side while Vince, Bernie, and Vicks stepped over toward the window to her right. Through the bars, they could see the helicopter gradually descending.

Vicks turned to Susan and said, "For the warden?"

Enraged to see the aircraft making its arrival, Susan didn't respond, instead keeping her gaze straight ahead on the outside.

"Yeah, must be. The boss shows up every morning in that damn thing. Who else here makes their commute from home to work in a whirlybird?" Fredericks replied. "Man's fuckin' ridiculous." He let out a chuckle and shook his head.

As the helicopter's landing skids made contact with the ground, Captain Groves could be seen among the outdoor perimeter lights walking out from beside the exterior of cellblock B and toward the helipad, which was located just outside the perimeter fence at the back end of the prison. He stopped, turned back toward the prison, and began to shout while waving his hand. He was motioning for someone to move ahead. Susan's group looked on, expecting to see someone appear from out of the side of the same cellblock, which Groves had emerged, but no one came. The advancing corpses were closing in on the aircraft, undeterred by its rotating blades.

Captain Groves ran back in the direction that he had just come from, disappearing behind the block. One of the creatures approached the helicopter from the side near the back. Lumbering aimlessly, the ghoul drifted into the tail rotor. Its left arm was lopped off at the shoulder, followed by the head being severed from the neck. Both appendages were hurled out into the surrounding grass field. The remainder of the body collapsed and instantly, after falling into the blades, was torn apart, dispersing blood and entrails into the open air in a forceful blast. Groves came darting out, forcing Warden Unitas along beside him with both arms.

"Figures," Susan muttered. She sighed heavily. "Fucking coward."

The two men made their way across the prison grounds and entered one of the security towers. Moments later they came rushing out through the door on the opposite side at the base of the tower, which led to the outside of the fence.

"They're gonna get swamped," Vicks said as more of the undead began to circle the aircraft "We should give them some cover."

"Bullshit," Fredericks replied. "You think we have enough ammo to do any damage?"

Vicks took a step toward him and squared up. "I wasn't talking to you."

Susan extended her arm and placed her hand on Vicks's shoulder, keeping him from moving any farther. "He's right. It wouldn't do any good."

He eased off and turned to her. "But that chopper could be our only hope of getting a message out. Who knows when anyone else will be—"

"Vicks," Susan interrupted. "We're staying here." She looked him in the eye with a stern expression on her face. He just stared right back, at first looking shocked, and then his expression shifted to disappointment. Her attention went back to the outside. Vicks scoffed at her disregard for his suggestion and then turned to join the rest of the group in their gaze through the window. The reanimated bodies continued to pour out from the surrounding woods as the noise from the helicopter blades traveled through the forested area.

Taken aback by the sight, Vince slowly stepped away from the window, where he had been standing next to Bernie, and then pressed his back against the opposite wall. He continued to stare out through the pane of glass with a blank look on his face. Bernie glanced over his shoulder after noticing movement from the corner of his eye. He saw Vince on the floor and quickly approached him. "Hey, man, you okay?"

"We're really going to die in here, aren't we?" Vince said quietly, trying not to bring any more attention to himself. "No point in hoping to ever see anything outside of those fences again. We're surrounded by death." Bernie let out a chuckle. Vince looked over at him, puzzled.

"Shit, I'm a lifer. As far as I'm concerned, hope was never an option," the older man responded. Gringo was listening in on the conversation from off to the side, near one of the windows farther down the hall. He lowered his head and gently nodded in agreement.

"They're almost there," Susan said as she watched the warden fall shortly behind Captain Groves.

With each shambling corpse that drew closer, Unitas's pace only slowed from fear and hesitation as he witnessed the number of decaying bodies grow. Groves approached the fuselage door and turned around after noticing that the warden was no longer by his side. His adrenaline had taken over after the sudden outpour of the undead, causing him to move ahead in a hurried pace. *Every man for himself,* Groves thought as he tried to find a justification for nearly forgetting about his colleague, surprised that the warden had practically become an afterthought in the tense moments leading up to their arrival at the helicopter. The creatures' movements became more rapid and intense as the warden appeared lost and vulnerable from his hesitancy; they closed in from all sides.

"Move your ass!" the captain shouted.

The abrupt command brought Unitas out of his disoriented state. He looked up at Groves, making eye contact, and then darted toward the aircraft with his eyes closed. As he rushed past each oncoming body within the vicinity of the helipad, the direction of the flesh-eating corpses slowly shifted, drawing them in toward the helicopter; and then gunshots began to ring out, loud enough to be heard over the whirling chopper blades. The warden flinched with each round that was fired off before throwing himself into the passenger cabin. Captain Groves lowered his pistol and swiftly followed behind, hopping into the cabin with his front side facing outward, allowing for a clear view of the surrounding area. He patted the pilot on the shoulder twice, and the helicopter began to gradually rise with the skids being lifted off the ground.

"Have you had that thing the whole time?" Unitas shouted over the chopper blades.

Captain Groves wiped the barrel of his gun with his sleeve and nodded his head, keeping his eyes on the firearm.

"Why didn't you use it sooner?" the warden continued.

Groves glanced up at Unitas, removed the clip from the pistol, and pointed out the shortage of bullets with a smirk on his face. The warden collapsed back in his seat with his head tilted back and let out an exhausting sigh.

Susan watched the lights from the helicopter gradually getting smaller as it drifted off into the night sky. Her eyes welled up with tears as her faith in the warden's better judgment was crushed by the harsh realization of the situation that was unfolding in front of her.

Vicks looked over at Susan and noticed that she was upset. "Are you okay?" There was a pause. He put his hand on her shoulder and said, "Hey..."

"I'm fine...let's get outa here," she said, turning away from the window and proceeded down the connecting corridor.

Vicks watched her walking away for a moment and then turned back to the three inmates. "Come on, guys, we gotta keep moving." The officer's eyes shifted back to the window to gaze outside. More of the undead appeared from out of the woods. The bodies closest to the prison joined the others, latching on to the perimeter fence—a horde began to form.

Cellblock A

Susan was leading the group when they approached the entrance door to cellblock A. Wasting no time, she grabbed the set of keys off her belt loop and proceeded to unlock the sally port door manually. Once unlocked she looked back at Vicks with a smirk on her face and said, "Hopefully, this time, the wait to get in won't be so long."

"Hey, I was tied up," Vicks replied, raising both hands in an attempt to further project his helplessness in the prior situation.

With one quick motion, Susan pulled back on the handle and opened the door completely. She stood beside the metal slab and said, "Everybody in."

Gringo peered into the sally port and slightly shook his head, hesitant to enter. "Nah, those guys are just going to lock us back up."

Fredericks scoffed and said, "No shit, ya dumb fuck, you're in prison."

"Hey, stop!" Susan said, raising her right hand to silence the guard. "Let's get in there, catch our breath, and we'll take it from there. I'm not even sure if we have any open cells available."

Gringo turned to Vince and Bernie with a distressed look on his face. Vince pulled himself out of his state of shock, placed his hand on Gringo's shoulder, and said, "Come on, you can't just wait out here in the hallway."

Fredericks grabbed Gringo by his upper arm and yanked him forward. "You're still an inmate in prison. It don't matter if the world has gone to shit or not…now move!" He threw the timid prisoner into the port and followed close behind. Vince looked at Susan, bewildered.

"He's right," she said in a partially defeated tone. "You three are still prisoners in this facility, and we as officers can't back down from our duty."

"And we respect that," said Bernie. "But that don't mean your guy has to treat us like pieces of shit. We've been cooperative the entire time." He broke eye contact and proceeded inside with the other two men.

Susan watched him pass by, wearing a remorseful expression. She looked at Vince, but he didn't say anything, knowing that nothing more could be said, and he followed Bernie in. Susan lowered her head as he moved through the doorway.

Vicks was next to enter. "Don't worry about it. Once we get inside, he'll be their problem," he reassured her, referring to Fredericks. "We're not even supposed to be on duty right now." He glanced down at his watch.

"It doesn't matter. We still have an obligation to keep this place in order," Susan swiftly responded. Vicks just nodded in agreement. She motioned her head and said, "Come on," and they were the last ones out of the group to go into the sally port. She shut the door behind her and made her way through the group of men up to the main entrance of the cellblock.

Instantaneous to her approach, a click echoed through the small space. The door had been unlocked. After a few moments, it began to open as the light from inside the block began to creep in through the crack and into the port. There was a man standing in the doorway. It was Officer Walsh, one of the other guards working the opposite shift from Susan, Vicks, and Fredericks.

"Officer Wells, we thought you were keeping an eye on cellblock B," said Walsh.

Susan didn't respond right away. She looked past the guard and into the block. There were inmates out of their cells, scattered throughout the large space—a sight similar to the one in B.

"We had to get out of there…too dangerous," Susan replied. She moved past Walsh as if in disregard of his presence. "What the hell is this?"

"It's all right, just giving the men a chance to stretch their legs," Walsh said. "They're playing nice."

Susan saw one of the inmates sitting on the floor against the concrete between two cells. She peered in closer, squinting her eyes and could see that both of his arms were extended out and limp on the ground. Beside his left forearm was a torn piece of cloth. She shifted her eyes over to his other arm and noticed a syringe resting in his hand. "Where'd the drugs come from?" she asked. Vince moved up just behind Susan and saw the inebriated man on the floor, recognizing him immediately. He rushed over to where the inmate was resting.

"Yes, go join them, feel free to explore the block," Walsh said as he watched Vince walk away. "All of you." He looked over at Bernie and Gringo.

Seeing that they were not going to be put back in cells, at least for the time being, Gringo did not hesitate and broke away from the group, venturing outward and in with the other prisoners. Bernie remained where he was, appearing wary of the situation.

"It's okay, Bernie, go on," Susan said in a reassuring tone.

He subtly nodded his head and proceeded by following Vince. As he was walking away, Susan glanced around the room and could see that Fredericks had already joined the two other guards on duty. Small talk had ensued between the three as laughter broke out. She sighed through her nose and continued scanning the large space until she was looking back, over her shoulder, where she saw Vicks standing by patiently. His attention was drawn toward Fredericks and the other two officers.

Susan turned back to Walsh. "What is going on?" she said. "I almost died back there, and you have these guys parading around in here like it's the goddamn circus."

"We have a way of running things on our shift that works, Officer Wells," Walsh replied.

"This isn't safe though. Do you even have anyone monitoring their drug intake?" She paused and then let out a nervous chuckle. "Jesus, listen to what I'm saying. This is fucking ridiculous!"

"How's he doing?" Bernie asked as he approached Vince who was crouched down beside the nearly unconscious inmate.

"He's in and out," Vince replied. The man's head swayed back and forth as he nodded in a lull from the effects of the opiate high.

"Maybe we should get him to his bunk so he can lie down."

"No. It's best we keep him upright in case he vomits. We don't want him to choke." Vince grabbed the inmate's shoulder and gave him a gentle shake. "Rodney, it's Vince. What do you say we get you up? I could use a rummy partner."

Rodney, the drugged-up inmate, rolled his head toward Vince with his eyes half open and a grin on his face. He said, "Ya know, being in here ain't so bad." Vince rolled his eyes, knowing that it was the heroin talking. Rodney continued. "I could stay here, just like this, for the next forty years." He chuckled, smacked his lips, and then peered up at the ceiling. His eyes were glazed over.

"What's your take away from all this?" Susan asked. "You got someone taking care of you on the outside?"

Walsh just smiled. "I'm taken care of on the outside…as long as I take care of these guys?"

"Family member of one of the inmates?" There was a pause. "I wouldn't take you for much of a drug peddler, Officer Walsh.

He looked at Susan, taken aback by the confidence in her accusations. "I think you should probably go home." He took a few steps toward her, imposing with his stance.

She nervously swallowed but stood her ground. Vicks moved a couple of steps forward and squared up. "Back off, Walsh."

Susan looked at Vicks and slightly raised her hand. "It's okay." She turned back to Walsh and said, "You know I can't do that. These men need to go back to their cells."

Off in the distance, one of the other guards overheard the conversation between Susan and Walsh. Vicks saw that they were drawing attention from others in the room and then noticed Fredericks mutter something to the fellow officer. The two guards, including Fredericks, began to approach. The third guard stayed behind to surveil the prisoners roaming the block.

"Everything all right over here?" the nearing officer asked. Susan looked the man over and saw that his name patch read "D. Benitez."

"Fine. Just informing Officer Wells of how we run things in here," Walsh replied. The three men looked at Susan as if she were an outsider to the boy's club, interrupting playtime.

"I can't let you guys continue to run the block this way," Susan proclaimed. "You don't know when these guys will make a move, and I assure you, they will."

Benitez scoffed and said, "Fredericks said you'd be difficult."

"No, she makes a good point—she doesn't need to worry, though…we've got it under control," Walsh explained.

Susan shook her head and began to gradually drift farther out into the block among the prisoners. "All right, I'm going to have all of you make your way back to your cells," she said out loud, rotating slowly to ensure that her voice was heard by everyone. She had the attention of the entire room, but the inmates remained where they were and just stared at the female officer as Walsh crept up behind her with subtle movements.

"Susan, look ou—" Vicks shouted but was abruptly stopped.

Susan hit the ground after being pistol-whipped to the temple from behind. Following the impact to the concrete floor, the momentum from the fall, combined with her dead weight, caused her to roll over from her side to her back. Many of the prisoners reacted with a collective groan.

"Goddamn it!" Vicks bellowed, struggling to lunge at Walsh. Fredericks and Benitez held him securely in place, restraining him from both sides.

Walsh glanced in his direction, appearing annoyed with Susan's interference and said, "Take her and the crew she came in with, and get them into individual cells."

Benitez gave a quick head nod and then cuffed Vicks. He shoved him into motion toward the empty cells closest by to their left. He looked at Fredericks as he walked and said, "Get the other two." He motioned his head over at Bernie and Vince.

Fredericks then nodded and made his way to the opposite side of the cellblock to collect the two men. As Benitez came up on Gringo, he grabbed the prisoner by his forearm, still having a hold on Vicks from behind with his other hand, and said, "Come on."

Fredericks forcefully pulled Vince up from the ground. "You heard him, move it."

With no hesitation Bernie began making his way over to the cells. Fredericks followed closely behind, having a tight hold on Vince.

"Keep an eye on him," Vince said to Walsh, trying to guide his attention toward the drugged-up inmate on the ground. "You have to keep him upright." He was pulled further away.

Walsh briefly acknowledged the request and then peered back down at Susan. "Be sure to put them in cells that are side by side," he ordered. "They can keep each other company. We don't want them getting lonely." He chuckled under his breath and then nudged Susan with the toe of his boot to make sure that she was out completely.

Internal Collapse

"That fence isn't going to hold," Gringo said to himself.

He gazed out of the small window from inside the cell he was being held in. From where the cell was located in the block, Gringo's vantage point allowed for a clear view of the prison grounds and perimeter fence on the outside. As far as he could tell, the entire facility was surrounded by the shambling corpses. The fencing began to gradually sway back and forth from the applied force of the advancing creatures. The sound of muffled moaning could be heard from the inside, collectively being emitted from the horde of decaying bodies. No one else in the cellblock seemed to notice. Gringo didn't say another word. He stepped away from the window and approached the bars, resting up against them. "How's Susan doing?" The question was asked more so out of boredom than genuine concern.

"She's still out, hasn't said anything," a voice replied from another cell. It was Vince. He was pacing back and forth in the small space.

"Bernie, you awake?" Gringo asked.

There was a pause and then a sigh emerged. "Yeah, I'm here, man." The weary inmate was lying down in the bed with his hands behind his head and his legs crossed. Bernie had realized early on that all he could do from inside the cell was rest his eyes and sit idly by. "How you holdin' up, Vicks?"

"I'm good. I'm doing good," Vicks responded in a calm tone. Steady breathing could be heard coming from his cell.

Gringo lowered his head, exhaled deeply and then looked back up to peer through the bars. On the opposite side of the cellblock, the group of guards were huddled together near one of the stainless steel roundtables located in the center of the room.

"She's still unconscious," Benitez said. "What if she doesn't wake up?"

Officer Walsh glanced over at the cell which held Susan and then looked back at the other three guards. "She'll be fine. Takes more than one hit to kill someone." He pointed to his temple. "My uncle was a boxer."

Benitez sighed and shook his head. "That's great and all, but what the hell are we going to do with them?" he asked impatiently.

"Watch it," Walsh responded quickly, raising his index finger up to the guard.

Fredericks stepped in to defuse the situation. "I say leave them in there. They're just going to cause us problems," he said. "They've been nothing but a pain in my ass."

"Slow down," Walsh replied. "We'll wait until she wakes up—have a talk. Hopefully for her sake, she'll be more understanding." He paused for a moment, looked at the row of occupied cells, and then continued, "The others seem to follow her lead."

"What do you mean?" Benitez asked. "Most of the group she came in with are inmates. Fredericks is right, we should keep them locked up."

"And we will," Walsh said. "Officer Wells though, she seems to have a pretty short leash on Officer Vicks. If we can reason with her…he should be no problem either." He peered past his fellow guards through the crowd of inmates and to the other side of the room where Rodney sat high as a kite. "Davidson, go check on our friend over there, make sure he still has a pulse," he said to the third officer as Vince's words from before ran through his head. "A death in the block may trigger one of these guys to act out, doped up or not. We keep 'em alive while sustaining their high, and things should continue to run smoothly."

Davidson looked over his shoulder at the inebriated man, shook his head with a disapproving chuckle, and then turned back to Walsh. "Got it," the stocky guard replied with a smirk on his face and proceeded to make his way over to the inmate. "Clear a path!" he shouted as he began to push through.

Several of the men barely moved at all, making just enough room for Davidson to get by. They looked at him, begrudgingly, with some appearing to square up. The officer moved ahead casually, unfazed by their intimidation tactics. He stopped about five feet in front of Rodney. There were two other inmates hovering close by. Once they saw Davidson standing there, they fled immediately. The officer stared the two down as they darted off; a stare that could have burned a hole right through them. He turned back to the prisoner on the floor and gave him a quick look over. Before Rodney's face had even come into view, Davidson had noticed in his peripheral vision that the intoxicated man's eyelids were fluttering. He shrugged his shoulders and said, "Yeah, he's still alive." Turning around swiftly, he made his way back to the group at the roundtable.

Sitting at the edge of the bunk, Vicks watched the guard go from one side of the cellblock back to the center where all of the roundtables were located. The officer rejoined his group and began talking among the others. Vicks could see Walsh listening intently. When all of the talking was done, Walsh peered through his band of guards and past the prisoners over toward the unconscious inmate on the ground. After a moment he turned to Vicks and their line of cells, looking him and his group over briefly. His attention then went back to the other officers, and no further action was taken after that point.

"Son of a bitch," Vicks said under his breath. He held a calm demeanor as he continued to breathe at a steady rate.

"They're scoping us out," Vince said.

"Wha?" asked Gringo.

"They keep looking back at us, planning."

"They're going to leave us in here to die," Vicks said abruptly. There was a pause. "Gotta get him back over here…distract them… something." His breathing intensified as his thinking seemed to become more erratic.

"Fuck, man! I told you guys we shouldn't have come over here!" Gringo replied. "What are you gonna do?"

"I'm going to kill him," Vicks responded with a snarled voice.

"Are you fucking kidding me?" Gringo said. "You really think we're gonna be able to do anything from inside these cells? They've got us out—"

"I know! I know! But we've gotta do something!" Vicks quietly shouted as he leapt up to charge the bars, losing his patience with the wary inmate. Once again the guards looked back at them. Vicks bit his tongue and clenched his jaw; there was a brief silence among the cells.

"Maybe we won't have to," Vince said.

"What do you mean?" Vicks replied.

Vince peered around the room at the other prisoners. "Their drug supply won't last. One of these guys will lash out. The order that those officers think they have will collapse on itself." He homed in on Rodney and saw that he was still sitting upright, but the movement of his eyelids had fallen flat. "It'll happen eventually. It's not like these guys became friends with the guards overnight."

"Yo, Walsh, you gonna play a hand?" said one of the prisoners sitting at the next table over. He was calmly shuffling a deck of playing cards. "I know it can't be easy losing all the time, but someone's gotta take you for everything you got." He raised his eyebrows, taunting the guard with his expression.

Walsh chuckled. "Consider it charity."

The inmate sat up straight and leaned forward. "The fuck is that supposed to mean?"

Walsh also sat up and leaned forward. He looked around the room. "Look where you're at. I don't really have time to be giving handouts…sorry." He shrugged with a smirk on his face.

"Asshole," the prisoner said under his breath.

"Don't take it personal, Sanz" Walsh said. "You're not the greatest card player. Maybe just work on your game for right now."

The prisoner didn't respond and went back to shuffling the deck of cards. Walsh just looked at the man, strangely fascinated with his response to what was said, almost as if he was feeding off the prisoner's inclination to shut down. *They're cowards,* he thought to himself. *All of them.*

"Have you seen it outside?" Benitez said, interrupting Walsh's train of thought.

Walsh turned back to the three other officers. "No," he replied. "But no matter, this is the safest place to be."

"Shyeah," Fredericks chimed in. "If things get any worse out there, soon, people looking for a safe house will be trying to get in."

Walsh nodded in agreement with the officer and said, "Well, unless the National Guard shows up, things continue to run how they have been—no one in or out."

A groan emerged from one of the cells. Vicks could hear that it was female. "Susan, are you awake?" he said, remaining seated as to not attract attention.

"Ugh, what happened?" Susan replied, struggling to lift her head off the pillow.

Vince rushed the bars and grasped with both hands. "Are you all right?"

"Wait, Vince," Vicks said in a short tone. "Just stay down, Susan. They've got us locked up. We don't want them back over here."

Susan's neck went limp, and her head collapsed back down into the pillow. "Why is my head throbbing?" she asked, caressing the side of her face with her right hand.

"Walsh knocked you out."

Susan sighed and then muttered, "Son of a bitch." Her arm flopped back down and lightly bounced off the bunk.

"You guys," Gringo said.

Simultaneous to the warning, Vicks saw Walsh stand up from the table to make his way over to their cells. "Shit," he said under his breath. Benitez and Davidson stayed behind.

Walsh approached Susan's cell with a grin on his face. "Officer Wells, good to see that you're awake and moving. I hope you don't take my course of action personal, all of you." He looked over to his left and then to his right, glancing over the other cells.

"Go to hell," Susan grumbled. She struggled to sit upright before throwing her legs over the side of the bunk. Propping her elbows up onto her knees, she began to nurse her headache by rubbing her temples with both hands as she peered down at the floor.

"So how do we proceed?" Vicks asked, turning to look at Walsh.

"That's up to you two," Walsh replied. "As I said before, we have a certain way of running things in this cellblock. If you don't like it, then you can stay locked up." He ran two fingers across the bars, and a metallic clanging noise echoed through the cell.

Susan looked over at the officer with her eyes clenched, reacting to the intrusive noise. "You know that any one of these guys will make a move the first chance they get. I knew you were an asshole, but I didn't take you for an idiot."

Walsh chuckled and then said, "One of your guys, maybe." He looked over at Vince, Bernie, and Gringo. Bernie was sound asleep, softly snoring. He turned back to Susan. "That's why they're gonna remain in their cells, but you two won't have to…if you work with us."

"Keeping 'em doped up will only work for so long," Vince interrupted.

"I wasn't talking to you!" Walsh quickly responded.

"He's right," Vicks said. "You've seen these guys come down before, they get restless and violent."

Susan slowly got up to her feet. She stumbled a bit, regained her balance, and then said, "They're just playing nice while you play their game. You gotta get them back in their cells, at least until things get sorted out there." She motioned her head to the window and then closed her eyes in pain from the movement.

Walsh shook his head and scoffed. "These guys are all talk. Besides giving them some freedom is the only way to keep them from lashing ou—" A burst of clamor erupted.

"Break it up! Hey!" Benitez shouted from behind Walsh on the opposite side of the room. Walsh jerked his body around and bolted toward the commotion without even knowing what was going on.

From where he was still sitting on the ground, Rodney had a tight grip on one of the other inmates, who was attempting to swipe the remaining dope out of his shirt pocket, both hands clenched tightly to his jumpsuit. Benitez lunged forward and grabbed the prisoner by his shoulder and the back of his collar, trying to split the two men apart. Davidson was just behind, taking no action rather shuffling in place.

"Get your ass over here, man!" Benitez shouted. He looked past the unavailing officer for more help, but Fredericks had vanished.

Unable to break free from the tight hold, the inmate looked into Rodney's eyes and saw that they had gone dead and cold—lifeless and blank. As Walsh approached, the inmate was violently pulled in closer. Rodney, or what remained of him, snapped forward, bit into his cheek, and then pulled back, tearing away a fatty portion of flesh. The injured man bellowed in agony, his pained scream traveling through the entire block. Walsh froze for a moment, hesitating from the horrific sight. In the midst of his hesitation, a hand reached around from behind and grabbed him by the throat, the grip being used as leverage to drive a shank into the back of his neck at the base of his skull. Walsh's body jerked from the penetration, and the blade went in deeper.

Walsh went limp, and the inmate began to guide him down to his knees like a puppeteer. The pull from his weight allowed for the shiv to be removed from the flesh with ease. Once on the ground, Walsh collapsed but caught himself with his left arm. Wasting no time, the prisoner swiftly thrust the crudely made knife into the officer's side, between the sixth and seventh rib, which punctured his lung. He repeated the motion, stabbing violently over and over until Walsh's breathing became labored and he fell forward. Lying face-down, more blood began to seep into his uniform. His body gradually became limp, and the last remnants of oxygen left his body, rendering him lifeless.

The bloodied shank was dropped in place, and the inmate walked away. Benitez glanced over his shoulder and saw Walsh, lying dead on the floor. When he turned back, still struggling with the two other prisoners, a second accomplice approached Walsh's body and then kneeled to remove the set of keys from one of the belt loops around his waist. "Davidson!" Benitez shouted. "Stop him!" He didn't respond, frozen in a state of catatonia. The inmate, with keys in hand, got up to his feet and rushed for the exit.

With Benitez's attention drawn away from the attack taking place in front of him, Rodney pulled at the inmate more aggressively, catching the officer by surprise, throwing him down in between the two prisoners. Unconscious from his wound and the loss of blood, the injured inmate fell limp onto the ground, causing Rodney to lose his grip. After being thrown into cell bars and hitting his head from the pull and momentum, Benitez rolled over onto his back, dizzy and disoriented. Before he could snap out of the daze and collect himself, Rodney, on all fours, threw his head forward and bit into the guard's neck, clamping down with intense force, allowing his teeth to penetrate the skin and sink into the muscle and flesh. The ravenous inmate began to thrash his neck, ripping deeper into the tissue, causing the fibers to tear. A fountain of blood erupted from the wound, followed by a steady, flowing stream of the red fluid. Seven seconds passed and Benitez was dead.

Davidson went to lean forward, on the verge of vomiting, when another prisoner charged the officer. Three expeditious jabs with a blade into his neck just below the chin and one forceful thrust into his chest caused the guard to stumble and fall to his knees. The blade was left deeply inserted, driven into his chest cavity. In a panic Davidson reached for the shiv and attempted to yank it out—the pain was too intense. He dropped his arm for a moment and took a couple of deep breaths. He raised his limb, once more, and then took a hold of the blade handle and began to pull. The process was slow and agonizing. He bellowed in pain until the shank had been completely removed. His hand shook uncontrollably, and he dropped the blood-soaked weapon. His breathing became labored before collapsing to the floor, facedown. Blood began to seep out and pool up from underneath him until he was dead. All the guards on duty in cellblock A had been taken out within a five-minute time frame.

Susan stood frozen in place, gripping the cell bars as she watched the inmates flee for the exit, following the man with the set of keys. Her eyes welled up with tears. The abrupt attack on the officers seemed to have jolted her out of the headache-induced daze that she had been in. She fell into a hypnotic gaze into nothingness. Vicks peered ahead at the bodies of the three guards lying motionless on the ground and surrounded by blood. A look of satisfaction washed over his face as any concern of their situation that he may have had before subsided. He grinned.

"Hey, get us out of here!" Gringo desperately shouted.

A couple of the of men among the pack of runaway inmates slowed their pace to look over at the row of cells after hearing the cry for help but were quick to keep moving as the others began to vacate the block, rushing out of the doorway which led outside and into the rec yard.

Vince's response to the events unfolding was one of silence. In his mind he had anticipated the fate of the group from the moment they had been locked up. No point in pleading, no point in even hoping. Gringo was right. *We shouldn't have come in here,* Vince thought to himself, getting lost in his cognition like most of the others at that point. From his understanding, a sense of acceptance washed over him, and he was at peace—he was okay.

Susan drifted back from the bars, gliding on the soundwaves of silence running through her head. Her calves hit the bunk, and she began to gradually sink until her bottom hit the mattress. She hung her head and closed her eyes.

Awoken from his slumber, Bernie was sitting upright on his bunk, hunched forward. He peered out through the bars at the gruesome sight, appearing disappointed but not surprised, knowing that the inability to listen would eventually get the guards in cellblock A killed.

"Goddammit!" Vicks shouted as the remaining inmates funneled out of the block. Within a matter of minutes, the entire room had been almost entirely emptied as the echoing chatter from the group of men faded with the last of them rushing out; all but the flesh-eating prisoner and the four dead bodies, some of which would soon be dinner before their turn. Vicks trudged over to his window and looked out up toward the sky. Infuriated, he began breathing heavily once again. A resonate metal clank rang out through the cellblock as the door slammed shut, and the reverberating uproar from the group of inmates was abruptly shut out—there was silence.

Susan raised her head, reacting to the loud noise. She peered over at the exit door for a moment before a sudden movement caught her attention from out of the corner of her eye. Her head jerked over to the left where Rodney's reanimated corpse was still feeding, but that wasn't what she saw. Her attention was shifted downward a bit, down to where Walsh's body was resting—motionless for a moment and then an elbow twitched. Susan flinched, caught off guard by the movement. She looked away, took a deep breath, and then turned back, gazing in horror as she realized that Walsh's corpse had begun the process of coming back to life. The throbbing pain in her head gradually returned. She lowered her face and closed her eyes.

Breach

The first rays of faint sunlight were beginning to break through and creep over the horizon line. Off in the distance, birds could be heard chirping away. Jose "Ghost" Romero, the man who had coordinated and carried out the attacks on the guards, flipped through each key from the guard's set with urgency, trying to decipher which one would unlock the gate leading into the prisoner transport pathway.

"Those fences won't hold much longer," he said to his right-hand man, Dante Benavidez, as the two of them cut through the rec yard and crossed the basketball court with the group of other prisoners following close behind.

With Jose holding the same status of power as Carlos did in cellblock B, the inmates naturally followed his lead, at that point, as if they were seeking his protection. The nickname "Ghost" was given to the man in power after going mostly unseen by the other inmates in the block while conducting his business affairs through the men working closest to him. After years and years of wielding his power with fear by using the men, Jose's dominating presence permeated through the block like a ghost; he was always watching without even being in sight, and with his white hair and beard, which he had obtained during his time being locked up, the name suited his appearance quite nicely.

As the group got closer to the perimeter fence, the line of reanimated corpses clenched onto the chain link became more agitated and physically active. The fencing began to sway violently, brought on by the continual applied force from the undead as they thrashed their paled, decaying limbs against the weakening barrier.

Dante looked over at Jose fumbling with the set of keys. He sped up his pace, moving ahead of the others, hoping to hint to Jose to move faster without having to say anything. Dante stopped and looked back, but no recognizable change occurred. Jose continued walking at the same speed, almost shuffling. The clamoring and moans from the creatures on the outside became louder and more invasive. Coinciding with the noise, Dante noticed that the trembling in Jose's hands became more apparent. He had been behind bars for nearly seventeen years of his life. As tough as he had been on the inside of the prison walls throughout the course of his sentence, the notion of stepping outside the prison fences scared the hell out of him, but in his mind, the walking corpses had not even been registered as a threat—it was freedom which was the threat.

Being overwhelmed by his anxiety, Jose wasn't even aware that his fear had been on full display for the men who had normally been accustomed to cowering at the mention of his name. His pace slowed even more, and the others gradually began to pass him. Jose kept his head down, attention still on the keys, but he ceased from flipping through them; he slipped into a daze until, eventually, he stopped moving forward. After reaching the gate, the other prisoners stopped and turned around. They looked at Jose, confused, not knowing what to do, and scared to say anything to him. They figured that he would snap out of it on his own, or so they had hoped.

Dante stood with the other men. He glanced around at all of them and could see the worry and bewilderment on their faces. The fence behind them continued to move, back and forth, but it was the smell of the decaying bodies which brought Dante back down. He looked over his shoulder at the creatures continuously pushing up against the chain link, and he then realized what needed to be done.

He approached Jose cautiously and extended his right arm, reaching out for the set of keys. Once Dante's hand came into sight, Jose reacted fast. Clenching the set, he jerked his arm back, grabbed Dante near his collar, and brought him in closer, thrusting one of the keys, placed between his index and middle finger, into his friend's throat. Blood spurt out from the wound and hit Jose in the face. The creatures' activity increased, and the fences began to sag. Some of the other inmates took it upon themselves to start climbing the fence which bordered the prisoner transport path.

Jose held the injured man and brought him down gently as his body fell limp after tensing up from the impact of the key puncturing his flesh. He ripped the key from Dante's jugular, and the blood flow became more rapid.

Nearly crawling on top of each other, the weight and force from the ravenous corpses caused the barricade to finally give way, allowing the bodies to spill over the collapsed chain link and pour into the grounds like a plague of vile locusts. Quickly the creatures stumbled up to their feet, and like moths to the flame, they went for the prisoners, some of which were still in the process of climbing the inner fence, ascending from the halfway point.

One man looked down at the advancing corpses and froze in place, hanging there like a live bait with his fear of heights not helping out his situation at all. Two of the undead monsters came up quick, grabbing on to the chain link once again while snapping their jaws up at the man, literally nipping at his heels. He felt a hand tugging at his lower pant leg, and he began to kick outward, frantically trying to free himself from the creatures' grasp. The inmate pulled his leg up with as much force as he could and then let the energy from the cadavers' pull guide his foot into the side of its head, exerting enough strength to push the monster back, releasing its grip. The prisoner scurried up the remainder of the fence and made it over the top. He didn't hesitate to let go, causing him to drop hard onto the graveled pathway.

On his knees and hunched over Dante's body, Jose's eyes shifted back and forth from the bloodied keys in his hand to the gushing wound on his friend's neck. His abrupt reaction, which led to the unintentional killing of his fellow inmate, left Jose in shock of how much control his fear actually had over him and how powerful it had become. The horde of walking corpses advanced on the inmate, but, unresponsive, he remained where he was at, kneeled beside the one man he was able to call a true friend while being incarcerated—and like most other things in his life, he had ultimately destroyed that as well.

The herd of decaying corpses enveloped Jose and the lifeless body of Dante. The two seemed to vanish in plain sight. The collapse of the fence brought more of the dead inward from the outside as they trudged over the fallen barricade and, in increasing numbers, entered onto the prison grounds.

Dark Days Ahead

The black was accompanied by a pulsating ring, which gradually dissipated. Susan opened her eyes, and in front of her, rabid jaws snapped at the cell bars. Without flinching or making any movement at all, she just sat there and stared into the eyes of Walsh's reanimated corpse—bloodshot whites not yet affected by corneal clouding though his skin was void of any natural color. The creature had both arms extended through the openings, reaching for the officer, but Susan remained unafraid as she became transfixed with the unnatural sight.

"Fuck! Fuck! What do we do!" Gringo shouted. A reanimated Davidson terrorized the hysterical inmate from the base of his cell. He was braced against the back wall of the small space.

"Just calm down," Vicks replied. "They can't get to us from out there."

"What the hell is wrong with them?" Gringo asked.

Speaking from prior experiences, Vince chimed in. "I don't know, but as long as we're in here alive, they won't stop." There was a brief silence. "They'll just keep coming."

"Vince, ya doin' okay over there, brotha?" Bernie said.

"Nah, man, I'm good, I'm good." Ridden with his anxiety, Vince looked away from outside of his cell and casually walked over to the small window, which looked out into the rec yard. He peered through the grimy-looking glass and saw that the perimeter fence was still intact on their side but saw none of the creatures nearby. *Probably on those guys like white on rice,* he thought to himself but didn't say anything to the others.

"This is fucked!" Gringo blurted out. He was pacing back in forth. "What if no one comes for us? What if—" He began to hyperventilate. "I'm havin' trouble breathing."

"Just relax. Someone will come for us," Vicks reassured him. The inmate who had been killed by Rodney was at his cell, exhibiting the same exact behavior as the others—arms extended between the bars and into the cell, reaching for the officer. At that moment he understood the seriousness of the epidemic as he stared it right in the face. A strong sense of concern for their situation came over him as if he had just had a sudden, overwhelming epiphany. "Susan?" She didn't answer. "Officer Wells!" He shouted. "What are we going to do?"

Susan was entranced with the teeth of the ghoul repeatedly biting at the air with no letup or ease in its attempt to attack. She fell deeper into her hypnotic state, with her gaze piercing through the mindless corpse. And then movement could be seen coming from the back-left corner of the cellblock. She turned her head. Fredericks came stumbling out of one of the cells looking lost as if he was a stray puppy, scared and in shock.

Susan jumped up to her feet and lunged at the bars, grasping them tight. The ghoul reached for her ankle. After noticing the extending arm, she pulled her leg back and kicked down on the appendage, fracturing the bone of its forearm on the metal piece running horizontal to the bars. She looked back up and shouted, "Hey!" Fredericks didn't respond and continued to move toward the exit. "You piece of shit!" Susan continued, "Get us out of here!"

Fredericks paused in front of the cells for a moment and looked over in their direction. The only thing that he chose to see were the undead bodies in front of their cells. He began to make his way for the door again, and his pace quickened. Susan's shouting had kept the creatures drawn in on her group, allowing Fredericks to pass through with ease.

"Fredericks!" Vicks yelled. "Get us out of here! Fredericks looked over once more, and while being distracted, he tripped over the transformed body of Rodney, who was feeding on the flesh of

Officer Benitez. The fumbling guard regained his balance and finally made it to the exit.

After having its feast interrupted, the dead inmate ceased from eating and gradually began to rise up from the ground; blood and viscera dripped from its maw. With a slow, unstable motion, the creature fell into pursuit of the fleeing officer, leaving the body of Benitez behind. It wouldn't be long before he would make the turn.

Fredericks removed the set of keys from his belt loop and, without realizing that he was being hunted, proceeded to unlock the door. When the lock was unlatched, he pulled the metal slab open and swiftly bolted through the opening, exiting the block. Before the door could close itself, the ghoul charged forward and lost its footing, collapsing onto the floor at the base of the doorway. Within inches of closing, the creature's hand had caught the rectangular metal piece as its torso hit the ground. The door was pushed open once more, and the reanimated inmate pulled itself through, using its left hand which was clutched to the lower door frame. Pushing off its forearms and getting onto its knees, the corpse gradually rose up to its feet as the slab was pushing up against its body. The rate at which the door was closing decreased, and the creature was able to make it out of the cellblock with little trouble. The metal piece came to a stop just before it could shut completely.

Vince pulled back from the bars and trudged over to his bunk. He sat down, and with his loss of hope, his posture became limp. Tears welled up in his eyes. The notion of dying inside the prison was becoming their reality. He let out a sigh of defeat.

Bernie eased back into his pillow and just closed his eyes, calm and content while going with the flow.

"Kinda hoping those guys make it off the grounds," Vicks said.

"They get picked up, and the cops send someone out here," Susan responded, finishing his train of thought.

"Right," Vicks said and exhaled, feeling overthrown by the circumstances.

"This is bullshit," Gringo blurted out. "You guys work here. Pick the locks…something!" He had remained in his state of panic.

"Picking locks isn't exactly a part of the training," Vicks replied. "We're not going anywhere."

Gringo didn't say another word. As if he were a five-year-old boy throwing a temper tantrum in succumbing to the situation, he plodded over to his bunk and dropped down hard. The group fell silent.

"Thank you for sticking with me," Susan said amidst the quiet. The inmates didn't respond, assuming that she was addressing her fellow officer. "You're good men, all of you," she continued. "You wouldn't be in those cells if you didn't have my back…he would've kept you out there with the others."

"Of course," Vicks replied, and the large empty space fell silent once more. There was not much else that could have been said. Vince, Bernie, Gringo, Vicks, and Susan sat in their cells, absorbing the quiet as a group, knowing that everything they had done was with the sole intention of doing the right thing.

Vince continued to look out of his window, seeming to have found some peace of mind. Bernie's light snoring could be heard by the others after he had drifted back into a deep sleep with ease. Gringo scanned the cell, desperately looking for anyway to escape, and then he turned to look down at his bunk, noticing the bedsheets. He peered up at the bars, which were built into the windowsill, from top to bottom and, with his eyes shifting, roughly measured the length from the window to the floor.

It will work, the hopeless inmate thought to himself, and he didn't speak another word.

The undead on the outside approached the penitentiary, closing in on the two cellblocks. The grounds had been overrun by their overwhelming numbers, which had reached the triple digits, and still the size of the horde continued to increase.

It wouldn't be long before the interior of the penitentiary became infested and the structure of the prison be dismantled completely, both in its physical state and in the state of its order.

About the Author

Dustin William Miller was born on May 18, 1987, in Albuquerque, New Mexico. He discovered his interest in writing when he was in the fourth grade after picking up a copy of *The Lost World*. He cites the author, Michael Crichton, as the main inspiration in his writing journey.

CPSIA information can be obtained
at www.ICGtesting.com
Printed in the USA
FSHW010948080120
65866FS